Feeding the Wolf

Brian C. Holmsten

To Jeff

Thanks for encouraging me to go on this wild, crazy ride —
and sticking with me until it was complete.

"The truth is, unless you let go, unless you forgive yourself, unless you forgive the situation, unless you realize that the situation is over, you cannot move forward."

Steve Maraboli

Friday, October 17

I was blissfully asleep, dreaming of children playing with colorful bundles of balloons, when the scene was rudely interrupted by Buddy Guy singing. It didn't make sense, the song juxtaposed with the kids, until I became aware that it was my iPhone alarm ringing. I opened one eye, then the other, and reached for where I had left the phone. I found it, picked it up and started pressing all over the screen hoping I'd find the sweet spot that would silence the music. It worked, and Buddy had the blues no more.

It was early and I was tired, but this was not the day to be hitting snooze or dragging my feet. As my friend Dan had said last night, my whole life was leading up to this day, and I supposed he was right, although it seemed as though I spent a whole lot of time taking detours and exploring the sights to get here. And the ironic part of "being here" was that I was leaving here. Which I would get about doing once I got out of bed and got myself ready. Hence the alarm wagging a loud finger at me on a non-work day.

I jumped out of bed, shuffled to the bathroom, turned on the shower, waited for hot water to flow, and stepped in. A few minutes later I grabbed my towel, and a few more minutes later I was dressed. I wasn't going to spend time on this today, no shaving or anything, just the basics. Bed to shower to dressed, maybe ten minutes. Probably a new record for me.

I did my tenth "final" check of my bag and made sure I had everything packed, and then did a final exhaustive inspection of my room. Nothing left under the bed, in any drawers, in the closet. Nothing hiding. Feeling as confident as one can prior to morning coffee, I grabbed my bag, clicked off the light, and left the room. No need to get sentimental; it was a random hotel room, two nights, nothing special. Leaving that room was the easy part.

There was coffee in the lobby, which I gladly helped myself to. As I waited for it to cool enough for a sip, I checked the weather on my phone. The forecast called for bright sun, cool temps, and no rain. Thankfully, instead of throwing a typical Midwestern hissy-fit, Mother Nature would be blessing us with what some call a "picture perfect autumn day." So at least I had that going for me. Sure as hell beat slogging through rain or, god forbid, snow. I took a careful sip of the coffee – oh man, so damn good – and walked out into the cool morning sunshine.

I had packed the car the night before; at least, I had packed everything remaining that wasn't essential (that stuff was in my bag), or that I hadn't already shipped ahead. So in theory, I was ready to roll. But nothing like this is ever quite that easy. I was leaving the city where I grew up, where I married, where my marriage subsequently failed, where I made plenty of good and bad choices, where I still had a sister and nephew and mother and plenty of friends. I had one friend call what I was doing a "do-over," while another snidely said I was running away. Whatever. To me it was simply starting over, starting anew.

Chicago is a huge, sprawling city that moves quickly and assaults your senses. It's intimidating to some, comforting for others. Some days, I felt as though it wasn't possible for me to exist anywhere else. The city was so familiar to me; the rhythmic rumble of the EL trains, the acrid odor of the sewers during the hot summer months, the musty scent of Lake Michigan after the rain, the obtuse orchestra of car and truck and cab horns as they blared and argued while stuck in traffic. Other times, the city felt like a foreign land, and it could become very easy to feel lost and alone amongst your three-million neighbors. Hell, seven-million neighbors, if you counted (or lived in) the suburbs that seemed to extend to Iowa and beyond. It could be very impersonal – right up until some moment when you meet someone new in a corner bar in some nondescript strip mall in a far-off neighborhood, and find out he's from the same neighborhood as you, or their cousin went to high school with you, or their dad bowled with yours. And at those times the flavor of the city took on nuance and texture and spice, and . . . .

And it didn't matter. It was time for something new.

This time of the morning meant there would be traffic, which was nothing new. Chicago rush hours are notoriously brutal. It often took a commuter over an hour to drive 10 or 12 miles from the burbs to the city. And by this point in time there were just as many people reverse commuting from the city out to the suburbs, so no matter where you were, or wanted to go, it was going to take you a while to get there. I pulled my old Toyota Solara out of the hotel lot and joined the fray, hoping that my state of mind would be different enough from my fellow drivers to allow me to relax about the next 60 minutes spent crawling, bumper-to-bumper, up the Kennedy Expressway, rather than be semi-consumed with the road rage that was, pardon the pun, all the rage these days. Just last week someone shot at a cabbie who used the on-ramp to pass stopped traffic; the guy at the front of the line who was cut off wasn't exactly pleased about it, and he let his .32 talk for him. And of course, the cabbie shot back. I hope the fare got a discount.

As I slowly passed the familiar exits and landmarks, I wondered how long it would be until I ever saw them again – if ever. I mean, this was a bit different than moving to Naperville or Schaumburg or some other suburb. You live 25 miles outside the city, you can still make trips in, see friends, take in shows or concerts, and if you're lucky score some Hawks tickets. You might not see the signs or streets or familiar haunts as often, but if you wanted to they were there. Not easily accessible, but available. But moving a bit farther away than the suburbs – moving out-of-state, across the country – that meant seeing these familiar faces would take an effort. And money. And time.

And willingness to come back. Take old clothes out of the closet and see if they still fit, or are still in style.

My car slowed, then stopped along with the traffic just as I neared the sign trumpeting the Addison Street exit. Which was either ironic or poetic, since I had spent my last night in the city at a restaurant just down Addison, in the Lakeview neighborhood. An old haunt, one I'd been to many, many times over the past dozen years. Intended to be a going away fete, it flowed in turn from happy to maudlin, changing in time with the amount of alcohol consumed and the need for someone (anyone) to unburden him or herself of their wishes for me, past or present. My friend and business partner Dan had organized it, and he invited most of the people who were in our circle of friends. I had resisted, mostly because I wasn't in the mood to have a night of tears. Dan had insisted, since, as he put it, "Don't be a prick, you may never see some of these people again, and you at least owe them a chance to say see ya later, especially since you're the only person in the western Hemisphere not on Facebook and they'll have no way to keep in touch with you once you're gone." I mentioned that my email wasn't changing, and anyone under the sun could email me, or since my cell wasn't changing they could call me or text me, but that went nowhere, so the party was had.

It was well into the evening when I found myself at the bar, nursing a Four Roses on the rocks, when Elena jumped up on the stool next to me. She and I had known each other from work for maybe 10 years, and it had always been a friendship that included liberal flirting and innuendo, and we teetered on being FWBs as much as BFFs. In fairness, I had been married for most of those years, rendering my flirtations harmless. But she was happily single and vocally available, and when my marriage crumbled she was the first on the phone offering to help, listen – whatever.

She put an arm around me and smiled, her deep, dark eyes filled with sadness and chardonnay. Her brown hair was now short, framing her petite face more carefully than the long curls she sported in the past. She didn't say a word, just looked into my eyes, a slight smile fighting her lips.

After a long twenty seconds she broke the silence. "You're really doing this, huh?"

I nodded. "Yup. Done deal. House sold, life packed and shipped," I smiled at her, took a sip. "I have half a tank of gas, it's late, I'm wearing sunglasses, it's . . ."

"Oh shut the hell up," she said, and slapped my shoulder. "This isn't the Blues Brothers, this is fucking real. You're leaving. You're leaving us. You're, . . . do you realize what you're doing?"

"Yes I do," I swiveled the old chrome and vinyl stool to face her, "I have some idea of what I'm doing."

"Well it's a fucking bad idea."

"Oh c'mon," I said, getting a bit defensive. "It's not like I haven't . . ."

"Oh, I know, I know," she said, picking up her glass of wine and draining the final golden drops. "I just, . . ."

"What?"

She leaned heavy on her left elbow on the bar, and looked at me. "I just feel sometimes like life is getting away from me, like, . . . like, things, people, you, are progressing, changing, moving forward, and it feels, especially right now with you taking off, like I'm watching it all as I sit still, and I'm still the same except each morning I find one more wrinkle below my eyes. I mean, Christ, Shannon got married last year, Peter two years ago, Colleen Regent moved to Nashville to marry her boyfriend . . . you think it's spring or summer, and suddenly you wake up and it's winter and cold as hell out there and you're all alone under a blanket watching reruns of Cheers with your cat." She turned and placed both elbows on the bar, her head dropping to rest in her hands. "I'm not ready, I'm not liking, . . this whole . . . ."

She stopped, fell silent for a moment, then turned her head to look up at me. "Getting old sucks."

"Me leaving is not going to make you old."

"I know," she said, "but it's just something else happening in life, another marker, and soon it'll be a distant point in time, 'oh, remember when Wade left, back when we were all so young,' that sort of thing, and it's making me feel old already, before it even happens."

"Oh, c'mon," and I leaned over and wrapped my arm around her shoulder, "you are not getting old."

She smirked. "We're all getting old, haven't you noticed?"

"Getting older, sure, but not old, like 'old old' if you follow. No, we're not in our 20s anymore, but we're not lining up for the blue-hair special at Denny's either."

"I'm feeling old," she said.

"You don't look old, you look great." The moment I said that, I immediately wished I had chosen some other words or phrase.

She straightened up. "Oh, really." She leaned closer, and looked directly into my eyes. "So how old do I look? Still young enough that you'd notice me in here if you didn't know me?"

"Oh come on, you know . . ."

"Know what?" She asked. After a far-too-long five seconds of silence between us she continued. "Know that I at least used to look good enough for us to flirt almost every time we saw each other? Know that there were times when I made sure you knew what I was thinking, and that I was here if you wanted?" She sat back and brushed her hair off of her forehead. "How come we never got together?"

"Well, for starters, I was married, remember?"

"Oh I remember," she quickly shot back. "And it was sweet how you stayed married, even when everybody knew you really weren't emotionally married any more. But you haven't been married now for what, almost 2 years? And even before that, there were a lot of nights, events, whatever, where you sure didn't act married. You spent a lot of time acting very available. I mean, I was damn sure at some point we'd end up together, at least for a night if not longer. How come I never got a chance?"

The bartender made an abrupt appearance. "Miss, another glass?"

"Please," Elena replied, pushing her empty glass toward the back rail of the bar. She then turned her attention back to me. "You know, you played the game, but then never played the game, if you see what I'm saying. So what was the deal, I'm okay enough to flirt with and maybe get your kicks that way, but not okay enough to take to bed?"

"Geez, Elena, stop it."

"No, no, you tell me, what's it always been about me, what is it with us?"

I put my hand over hers as it rested on the bar. "First, if I never knew you, I'd always notice you in every room I ever entered where you were there."

"Yeah, right."

"No, listen," I said, "are there times I wanted to follow through on our playfulness and suggestiveness and flirting and all that? Hell yeah. But we've been friends first, I mean when we met and I was married we hit it off and were friends, and over the years yeah, I've had a hard time, pardon the pun, being friends with a really attractive woman, which is what you are."

"But," she said.

"But," and I sighed, "I was truthfully scared that doing anything with you would screw up us being friends."

"Oh shut the fuck up," she replied, and reached for her fresh glass of wine that had silently landed on the bar. "Don't give me that, 'I didn't want to sleep with you because I didn't want to ruin our friendship' thing, I've seen it happen and sometimes something great comes of it, and if not and the people want to stay friends, they find a way to stay friends."

"No," I said, "stop, stop . . . listen, did I want to? Hell yeah, over the years there were plenty of times I wanted to grab you and carry you to the nearest bed, or backseat, or wherever we could've done it. But first,

I was married during a lot of those years, and whether happily nor not, I was married. And second, I've always liked you too much for you to be a fling while I'm married, or when I'm confused and not sure what I'm doing, or to feel like I'm taking advantage of you with something I can't emotionally back up, and I, . . . I see you and look at you and to me you're more deserving than that."

We sat in silence for about a minute. She sipped her wine, I drained my bourbon. And I thought back to the first time Elena and I had met, at a Christmas Party for my work maybe 10 years earlier, held at a restaurant in Chicago's trendy near north area. She was there with her then boyfriend, I was there with my wife, Sarah. It would have been difficult not to notice her – she was rather striking with long, dark curls, stylishly red-framed glasses, and a blouse that looked as if made from silver tinsel. She laughed easily, throwing her head back and letting her curls drape over her shoulders. While Sarah and I drifted left in the room, Elena and her guy drifted right.

I grabbed drinks for Sarah and I, and then we spent time talking to my co-worker friends. Sarah knew them, to a point; she had heard me speak of them often, and she had come with me when my manager had a summer barbeque, but she wasn't what you'd call "friendly" with them, nor was she inclined to leave my side and strike up conversations on her own. Where I went she followed, whom I talked to she listened to. We moved through the party as a pair. Right up until she whispered in my ear, "I need to find a restroom."

"I believe they're over there," I said, nodding toward the hallway leading to the rear of the room.

"Oh, okay," she said. "Get me another glass of rosé in the meantime?"

"Sure thing," I said. She wandered toward the restrooms, I made my way to the bar. When I reached it, Elena was accepting a glass of white wine from the bartender. She turned with it and almost bumped me as I found my spot.

"Oh, God, sorry," she said. Then, without hesitation, she offered her hand. "Hi, I'm Elena. And you are?"

"Wade, hi, nice to meet you."

"You too," she said. "And why are you here? Worker bee or spouse?"

I smiled. "Worker bee. I'm a writer in the marketing group."

"Fun stuff. Oh, wait, Wade? Sure, I think Kevin mentioned you, that's my brother, he's a PR guy or something like that, . . ."

7

"Oh, yeah yeah, Kevin Rogers, right? He's your brother?"

"Yeah, that's him, I think you guys cross paths every now and then or something like that."

"Yeah, I did something for him a few months ago." I paused. "So, what brings you here? You're not a worker bee with us are you? Or are you, just in a different area."

"I'm a freelance worker bee, I'm a graphic designer, just worked on something for Kevin, . . ."

"Nepotism works," I interjected.

"Yeah, ha ha, no, but really, Kevin hired me for something last minute, he couldn't get his usual vendor to do it, so he used me. And as a thanks, he invited me to the party. And here I am."

"Whatever gets you free food and drinks, I'm good with that." I turned to the bartender and ordered a glass of rosé and a Sam Adams.

"So," she said, "you're a writer, huh? Any good at it?"

"I like to think so," I said. "It is what it is, writing marketing crap for an investment company."

She nodded her head and took a quick sip of her wine. "So, are you one of those writers who secretly has a novel in the works? Just doing this until you're rich and famous?"

"Ah, no." I said. "Would be nice, but no novel. Just this."

"Still time," she replied. "So, you here by yourself, or do you have a significant other lurking somewhere?"

"My wife's finding the restroom, so, . . ." I held up my left hand, ring in place, "taken. You?"

"Single, here with a friend, enjoying the hell out of life. I actually can't imagine being married yet. Someday would be nice, but right now," she leaned closer, "I'm just having fun when and where I can."

"Nothing at all wrong with that," I said. "Enjoy being young while you're still young." The bartender set our drinks down, and I pulled out my wallet.

"Well, you get your drinks for you and the missus, and maybe I'll see you again sometime," Elena said. "Maybe if I do more work for my brother our paths will cross again in a non-bar setting."

"That would be great," I said. "Always looking for designers."

She pulled a business card from her purse, leaned toward me, and slipped it into my open wallet. "In case you ever need me, now you can find me." She smiled, turned, then started walking away. After maybe four steps she turned back toward me and winked.

I smiled and grabbed the glass and bottle, just in time to hear Sarah ask, "So who was that?"

"Oh, her brother works with us, she does some freelance work. Just chatting while waiting for the drinks."

Sarah took the glass of wine from my hand. "Chatting, huh? You seemed to be enjoying the chat. And she certainly seemed to be enjoying chatting with you."

"Never met her before tonight," I said, "and besides, it's a Christmas Party, people tend to chat with other people when standing around the bar waiting."

She smiled. "And who wouldn't want to chat with the cute guy at the bar, right?" She gave me a quick peck on the cheek, grabbed my hand, and led me away from the bar. "Maybe you can chat with me for a while," she said.

I didn't cross paths with Elena the rest of the evening, but she did more freelance work for our group after the New Year, including work for the same project I was on. And the friendship took off from there. After a few years my friend Dan went as far as refer to her as my "work wife."

I was thinking about the various projects we had worked on over the years, the conferences we both attended, the parties, events, gatherings with friends. I was replaying our history in my mind, right up until her voice brought me back to the moment, us at the bar, me ten hours from leaving town.

"While I appreciate you not wanting to use me, I'd also have appreciated you giving me the chance to decide myself what I'd want to feel with you." And then I saw her eyes turn wet. "And damn-it, now you're leaving, and the best years we had together, or we could've had together, are gone, and you're leaving forever and we'll never know if there could've been an 'us' or not, even for a short time."

All I could do was hug her. I wrapped my arms around her, and she wrapped hers around my shoulders and back. "I'm sorry," I whispered, "I really never wanted to hurt or anger you."

"I know," she said softly, "but this just makes real. And part of me hopes you regret it one day soon, what we could've had or could've been, and a deep, dark part of me likes to think you'll be there alone, wishing I was there, knowing you could've had me any time you wanted, . . . "

Before she could finish a hand grabbed my shoulders and a voice boomed. "Hey, get a room, get a room." We separated, and standing with us was Steve Healy, another member of our long time "pack." He was holding a bottle of Bud, and had the unsteady stance of one who had finished plenty of Bud's buds.

"Steve," I said.

"Hey, not interrupting anything I hope," he replied.

Elena wiped a tear. "No, just letting this idiot know that I'm going to miss him, and I wish he wasn't going anywhere. Hi, Steve."

Steve put his other arm around her, squeezing us against both sides of himself. "Yeah, this guy, he's doing what we all kinda wish we could do, right? Do over, start again, head for the hills and begin fresh, amiright?"

"Well, not quite that easy," I said. But Steve was off following his own train of thought.

"Yeah, I tell ya, it takes guts to leave the city where you grew up, where you have family, only place you've ever know, and go somewhere else," he slurred. "Not sure I could do it."

"Uhm, you know Elena isn't from Chicago, right? She came here from what, Indiana, after college, right E?"

Steve squeezed us harder, closer. "Indiana, that's a few miles away, it's almost local."

I stepped out of his grasp, amazed at how strong his paws still were after that much time spent imbibing. "Southern Indiana, Steve. She was raised closer to Kentucky than Chicago. Whole 'nother planet."

"So anywho," continued Steve, "where ya headed? Someone saying Arizona or something?"

"He's headed to Sedona," said Elena, "aren't ya? Beautiful rocks in the middle of nowhere."

"Sedona? Never heard of it," said Steve. "Near Phoenix?"

"Nope," I replied, "farther north, mid-state."

"What's in Sedona, a woman?" asked Steve. Elena smacked his arm.

"Naw," I said, "chasing gold. Hoping to strike it rich."

"Really? That sounds cool," Steve said with childlike wonder in his voice.

"No, no, listen to this," Elena said, and she fumbled with her phone for a moment, pushing apps and icons. "I looked up Sedona a few days ago, this is what I found, listen.

"The road from Flagstaff to Sedona, 89A, is one of the most beautiful and most photographed roads in all of America. It slowly and methodically snakes its way down from the mountains of Flagstaff, through the bluffs and crags and valleys of Oak Creek Canyon, then weaves through parts of Coconino National Forest before releasing into the vibrant red rock formations that make Sedona unlike anywhere else in the world. It's an exhilarating 45 minute drive through twists and hills and some of the most gorgeous sights to be found anywhere."

She stopped and looked up at Steve and me. "Seriously, you're moving to a fucking travel brochure, it's probably not even real. It sounds like if Disney did wilderness or something." She put her phone in her pocket. "Really, you want to leave the city, this life, for a bunch of rocks?"

"I dunno," Steve said, "sounds kinda soothing an' peaceful to me."

"Sounds like the anti-Chicago, if ya ask me," she said. "I don't get it, but if you wanna go play out this 'mountain man, I'm alone in the rocks' fantasy, fine by me. Just remember, we'd rather have you right here, in the middle of life, the middle of noise, the middle of things happening, and the middle of your friends."

With that, Elena leaned past Steve and came close for one last hug. She put her arms around my neck, kissed my cheek, and whispered, "It actually sounds wonderful, that's how I know you'll never come back. But in case, I'm here if things don't work out, just call. I may still answer."

"Thanks," I said, "I know."

"Love ya, Wade," she said. "Always have, always will."

"Back atcha, E."

We pulled apart, and Elena said, "Excuse me guys, I need to find the ladies room." She turned sharply and cut through the crowd, and was out of sight within seconds.

Steve and I turned from where Elena was, and looked at each other. "So," he said, "she okay? Seems kinda upset you're leaving."

"Sometimes change hits when we're least ready, and I think she's nowhere near ready."

Traffic finally started to crawl. I let it pull me farther away from the city, the personality of the surroundings getting less intense and distinct. Soon I was almost going 45, fast enough to make me think I might make it to the suburbs before lunch, and make it to Missouri by dinner. If it was a late dinner. I fiddled with the radio station; I'd never been happier having satellite radio as I was now, headed toward three or four days of driving. No need to search for a signal in rural Oklahoma, or when passing though the majestic emptiness of New Mexico. The soundtrack to my mood could – and would – be set anywhere, any time. Whatever I chose.

Whatever I chose.

I allowed myself to get lost in thought as I drove. Well, not that I had to give myself permissions to think; it was more of, I gave myself permission to roll around in my mind not only last night, but all of the things that led up to last night. I had surrounded myself with my friends last night, sharing space with people who always had, and always would, put a smile on my face. Yet many of these people had only become important, become "friends," in the past five-to-seven years. They hadn't been there in high school, in college; they weren't family; they weren't friends that I had incorporated through marriage, or other couples we'd met in the course of being a couple. What I had done last night was surround myself with those who had provided an escape from family. Last night was only possible because of the fractures that permeated and soon came to define my marriage, and had driven me to seek more time with those with whom I shared work and career and interests outside of my home walls. Those were the thoughts I harbored as I drove: how perhaps I capsized the boat in order to allow myself to feel good about being rescued by people I liked and wanted to be with. I wanted to choose one set of people over the other, without really choosing, without disappointing anyone. And without the guilt that accompanies disappointing someone you loved.

As the buildings grew more sterile and less frequent, and the open land expanded between every off-ramp, I thought about Sarah, how we started, how we ended. It's such a cliché that nobody gets married thinking they'll get divorced, yet looking at our time together now it's hard to see how I ever thought we'd stay together. Three years dating, seven married; now, almost two years since we've parted, I kept thinking that there had to be a reason for it to have happened at all. Big picture, cosmic thinking, karma, fate, destiny – why did we get together if we were going to split apart? What was the point of those years, those months, those endless arguments and icy silences?

I hit my first exit, needing to swing south toward St. Louis. I was still in the Chicago metro area, but seeing the sign overhead – "St. Louis" – made me feel as though miles were being accumulated. It also made me think of a business trip from three years ago, when Sarah and I went to St. Louis for some work I had to do. I rarely ever brought her on business trips; she didn't want to miss time at her own job, plus my work, corporate writing, wasn't something that lent itself to fun, familial times when out of town. But in this one case we decided that she should come with. In my mind, I was thinking of it as a last gasp to try to save us, and I would have bet the farm that she was thinking the same thing. So we packed up the car and headed for 4 days on the outskirts of St. Louis.

Actually, now that I think about it, that's wrong: "we" didn't decide to make the trip together, I talked her into it. I could see – we both could see – that things were breaking down between us, so I thought perhaps time away would help. Turns out, we needed more time than a business trip would allow, and certainly more "together" time. "Oof," I said out loud to myself as I thought about it, "That was a huge mistake."

The drive down had been fine. Fiddling with the radio, small talk, nothing unusual for two people who had spent years together. But it felt forced, and the conversation was stale. We both knew that we were going down this road (literally and figuratively) trying to see if anything could be salvaged between us. As the minutes turned into hours the words dwindled, then evaporated. I'm not sure more than six words were said between us during the last hour of the drive, and as we pulled in to the Drury Inn in O'Fallon it felt as though we had traveled for days without seeing another living soul. We trudged into our room, where she immediately jumped into the shower, and I unpacked, fired up my computer, and looked over notes for my meetings the next day.

Dinner, the next day, the next . . . funny, I can remember bits and pieces of it, while other moments seem lost. Walking along the riverfront, ice cream at Ted Drews, . . . things we did that should have been filled with conversation, but instead was done in silence. My most vivid memory of the trip was dinner on the final night, at a small Italian restaurant that Yelp said was "Can't Miss!" in almost every review. Intimate, pristine white table clothes, perhaps the best bottle of Valpolicella I've ever had, still to this day – and two people who really had so much to say to each other but were too scared to say anything out loud, because if it were spoken out loud it would be real. And both of us

13

were afraid of what we were thinking and feeling, but neither of us wanted it to be real. Plus, neither of us wanted to own the guilt of how the other would feel once the words were "out there."

"So, this trip for work, has it been worth it? For work?" Sarah asked.

I nodded. "Yeah, it was a good idea for me to be down here."

Followed by silence. Then, "Well, good. Glad it's gone well."

I nodded again. "Yup."

The dapper waiter brought the plates, and we eagerly ate, knowing that having a mouth full of pasta means you can't talk. For about 5 minutes we concentrated on our meals in individual silence.

"At least we've had time for dinners together," Sarah said, following a rather ample sip of wine. She said it with an unmistakable edge to her voice, and it accompanied a look that was all ice and knives and contempt.

"Well, c'mon, you knew I was primarily down here for work. Not like I can let them pay for me to be here, then not show up each day."

"Well then why am I here? Why did you drag me along?"

"I seriously thought maybe getting away for a bit might be nice, someplace different to shop, different sights, just nice for the two of us to get away."

She let her fork drop to the plate. "Maybe I just had unrealistic hopes that, who knows, maybe we could've spent some time together, doing something – something other than eating dinner."

"Wait, we've done a few things, don't they count?" When she didn't answer, I continued. "Well," I said, "tomorrow then, I should be done by noon, what do you want to do? Let's find something together that we can do together."

"Forget it, I'm forcing you to do something you don't want to do. Just forget everything."

"Oh come on," I said, my volume rising, "don't *do* that, don't lobby for something, complain that I don't want to do something, and then when I offer to do something slap it away like you don't care, that's not fair. Don't play that game."

"You're making a scene," a suddenly uncomfortable Sarah whispered, "just be quiet and eat, okay? Just forget it and eat." She turned her attention downward toward her plate, and started eating with a focused determination, as if doing so would erase the previous two minutes of existence. I sat there, unmoving, and for a moment just watched as she

14

ate, paying no attention to me, the other guests, or anything outside the boundaries of her place setting.

Later that evening, as we were back at the hotel getting ready for bed, we made our way around the room as if we were planets, orbiting but never touching. After 30 minutes of this I sat on the bed and said, "Listen, this isn't getting us anywhere. I'm sorry if this week hasn't worked out like you had hoped."

Sarah kept her head down, buried in her book. "Whatever."

"Geez, I'm trying here," I replied, the agitation in my voice oozing.

"Really? Because it feels like you're going through motions, doing what you think you should be doing instead of doing what you really want to be doing."

"Wait, what?"

"Seriously," she said, "did you really want me down here? Did you really thing I'd have fun here, or that we'd have fun here? I mean, why am I here, when it feels like you don't want me here?" She threw her book to the floor as spoke, and let the words hang in the air as she stared at me.

"Well," I slowly replied, "I just thought it would be good for you, and for us, to get away."

"Jesus, Wade, this isn't getting away. This is same thing, different place. And the same thing is that you're here, but you're not here. It's like there's nobody behind your eyes. What's up with you? Why are you, . . . what's wrong? What's wrong with you?"

"I'm just trying to do something that will make you happy," I said. "I'm just trying, ..." And I let the words hang and the thought die, trying to figure out just exactly what I was trying to do. It struck me that what I was trying to do was give mouth-to-mouth to a dead body, but it didn't seem real, nor did it feel as though any words I could have said, or any gestures I could have made, would adequately express what I was thinking or feeling.

Of course, I knew exactly what I was thinking; I just couldn't bring myself to say it out loud, especially to Sarah. What I was thinking was that I was tired, so very tired, of living my life in order to please her. I was tired of our "compromises" being no more than me giving in in order to sidestep any fights or any disagreements. I was discouraged that most of the things I wanted out of life I had allowed to be put aside so we could "go after our dreams," dreams that I resolutely nodded my acceptance of every time plans were made or directions were given. And more than anything, I was frustrated – with her, but mostly with myself – for falling into this cycle of doing what I thought was right in order to keep her happy, no matter how unhappy it made me. By this time, after almost seven years of marriage, I had no idea what I really wanted for myself out of life, but I had a bad, nagging feeling that whatever it was, I wasn't going to find it married to Sarah. I felt as though "we" existed, but Wade no longer did.

And I wasn't about to say that to her; not in a St. Louis hotel room, not during a four-hour drive home, not ever. How do you tell your wife that you don't want to be her husband anymore?

So of course, after that week all I did was slowly, silently, pull even farther away from her, from us. I found more things to do with my work friends and more reasons to spend time elsewhere. Being a writer, when I was home I worked on some of my own projects, including the screenplay that I had started three times over the years but never finished, the screenplay Sarah derogatively named "Wade's Perpetually Unfinished Masterpiece." I wasn't angry, I was just there, taking up space. Physically in the room, but mentally and emotionally far away, creating my own reality in which I readily had a say in each action I took. I basically spent my time daydreaming. It was happier than facing the painful reality of real life.

It took me another eight months to get up the nerve to leave. Sometimes you jump; sometimes you need to be pushed. In my case it was neither. I simply finished what had been started a few years prior. I got up one Saturday morning took a shower, and started packing a suitcase. Sarah came into the bedroom, stopped, and looked up at me.

"What are you doing?"

I barely hesitated packing, looked up at her, and then resumed with my activity. "Leaving. Going away. I can't do this anymore, and I know that you're just as unhappy as I am, so I'm leaving."

"No, you can't just quit," she said.

"Quit? Quit what? We haven't had . . ."

"We're married," she said, "we have that, we have all the years together, you don't throw that away."

"Listen," I said, "we're broken, and I know it, and God I hope you know it. Memories aren't gonna fix us, us walking around each other in silence, going out of our ways to avoid speaking to each other isn't going to fix us, . . ." I paused and looked up at her. "Doing the same things we've done the past months isn't going to change anything."

"We can change, we can get help," she said, her voice wavering. "Please don't do this."

"I need to. I need to for both of us. I need to get away, take a breath, get some help, and see what it is that's making me feel like, like, . . ." I let the words hang for a second.

"Like what?"

"Like I've let myself down just as much as I've let you down. Like I've lost sight of what I wanted when we started out."

"We can still have what we wanted when we met, when we started out."

I shook my head. "I really don't know what I wanted then, and I really have no idea what I want now."

She walked to me and grabbed my hands in hers. "Then stay, and let's figure out together what you want, and how to make us better." She was crying now. "Just, please stay, and let's get you right."

"And see, that's the thing, I know I'm not right, but we're also not right – us, together, we're not right, you and me both." I pulled my hands away. "It just doesn't feel like there's room for me to be right, and for us to be right."

"Please, don't," she said, tears streaming down her cheeks.

"I need to," I said. I finished packing the suitcase, then turned to her. "I'll come back Monday when you're at work to grab the rest of my stuff." I walked past her, then stopped at the door. "This, this isn't . . ." I turned to look at her. "This is just right now, what I need to do. Just give me some time."

She was crying, her shoulders shaking. She didn't say anything, so I turned to leave. As I passed through the door, I heard her say, softly, "Just leave, Wade. Just go."

I dumped my things into my car, headed to Dan's house to crash on his couch, and tried not to think about the change I had just forced myself into accepting.

Of course, damned ironic thing nobody who ever gets divorced tells you about; for a while – months, maybe years, depends on the person – you'll see things, hear things, smell things that make you think of the good times you spent with your ex, and you'll instantly have feelings of regret and loss, feelings that you did the wrong thing. You'll never know when it may happen, and you'll never be ready for that sudden "wow, what have I done?" thought to hit you. And that's what I was feeling engulfed by right now, two years later, as I drove down the expressway. Melancholy for the good, to the point of perhaps creating warm memories that hadn't existed, all to fit the narrative my wounded subconscious was trying so desperately to craft and force feed me. I was so relived to be free from being coupled with Sarah that I was exposed to feeling loss over what we started out with and started building years ago.

And it was odd to feel loss, since I had never felt that loss during our last few painful years of marriage. My therapist, Dr. Wright, said that even though I was the one who pulled away and initiated the break, I would still feel the void of loss, and would need to grieve for what had ended, much as one would grieve the end of a life. At first I waved that away, instead enjoying the overarching feelings of relief and contentment that derive from freedom, and from not acting as though your every move was performed upon eggshells. But as days and months passed, I found myself pausing for moments of extreme sadness and emptiness and, especially, guilt, as though my arm were missing and it was my fault. Dozens of hours of deep conversation with the good doctor made me own up to those feelings, and more than that, own the sadness, the emptiness, the wound that was there. The only way a wound heals is to fully bleed before scabbing. Emotions work the same way. I had to bleed.

And bleed I did. I bled over many bottles of my favorite bourbon (as well as many bottles of sketchy, unknown spirits). I bled at night, watching television or movies. I bled taking walks alone through the neighborhoods I previously haunted both alone and with Sarah. And I bled – profusely – in the arms and beds of other women. I told myself I was healing, and a few of those women were motivated to help that healing along in whatever manner they could. But too many mornings after, all I could feel was the deep cut, and it was still there, open, staring at me, waiting for me to fall in. And I felt lousy for doing this to myself and to Sarah, as if it were entirely my fault, as if I alone had sliced open both our arms.

There were times – mornings, mostly – when I wondered if what I was doing was seeking out other forms of intense emotional releases just to ensure that I could still feel, just to make sure that I was still alive. It occurred to me one morning, as I rolled out of bed and accepted a steaming cup of coffee, that I had become numb to being numb. It was "the norm" for me to not feel anything, for me to be running on a flat line, and that any moment of knife-edged life was akin to a rebirth. Which justified my decision to leave, while simultaneously giving me pause to think about how I had been living in a world of grey fog for years.

But how does one really get out of that fog? How do you change yourself so that the new becomes the norm? Ahhh – now that's the million dollar question. And nobody seemed to have the answer.

So I thought back to an old philosophical question: are you impacted more by nature, or by nurture? Can't much jump-start change via nurture, so let's see what we can do with nature. Let's change nature. Let's change our surroundings. Let's go somewhere else, change the scenery; maybe that will help lift the fog. So that's why I stopped what I was doing in the middle of a Tuesday afternoon about three months ago, drove to Belmont Harbor, and walked along Lake Michigan for about an hour. Something, some voice, was saying, "to change, to find yourself, you need to look elsewhere, you need to put yourself somewhere else." With the breeze and the lake mist slapping me in the face, I decided to leave Chicago and start somewhere new.

And now I was on the road, headed west, leaving the physical environment behind while being immersed with memories of it. As if I couldn't divest myself fully from where I lived all those years, where I was born, raised, grew, laughed, cried, loved, and lost. I was leaving, but my life was following.

Well damn.

Minutes on the road turned to hours. Indiscriminate fields of corn and soybeans passed my windows, not so much marking time and distance as they were enforcing the fact that most of the Midwest looks the same. I could have been in Illinois, Iowa, Minnesota, Ohio - - who knew? Someone awakening in the backseat would have little idea of the exact location. Even the gas stations and fast food stops that dotted each exit were replicas of those from the previous exits. It doesn't help matters when your search for the new reveals miles and miles of the same.

Still . . . I occupied myself by working the radio to set a mood, avoiding the semis that steadily dotted the right lane, and sipping coffee from a travel mug while trying to not drip down my shirt. I passed signs trumpeting small towns, names I had seen on maps but had never experienced firsthand: Dwight, Cayuga, Chenoa, Towanda. Finally appeared a sign with a name I did recognize: Springfield. State capital. Halfway point from Chicago to the Mississippi River and the state of Missouri. I actually was making progress.

After living in or near Chicago all my life, I found that any other city that purported to be a "city" seemed awfully small by comparison. I had traveled to Indianapolis quite a few times, each time marveling at how I entered the "city limits" to a series of farms and corn fields, each a copy of the last, right down to the half dozen black and white cows that solemnly chewed grass while gazing past the wire fences. Milwaukee, same thing. Even flying and landing in cities like Memphis, Denver, Pittsburgh – you're in the city, and it doesn't feel like a city. To me, a city began about 30 miles outside the city, with the trickling of suburbs growing thicker the closer you came to the city, and those final "border burbs" indistinguishable from the city itself. On a map, Springfield, Illinois, is an important city, a state capital. Driving though it provides new perspective, makes you aware that this "city" is not an organic growth, but a social experiment in seeing how many people can tolerate living in the middle of nowhere. State Capital, state services, all those employees – and not much else. Take away the capital, and Springfield would turn out the lights and never turn them back on. Some city.

So Springfield marked time and distance, but it also marked notice to assess conditions. Meaning, perhaps this would be a good time to stop for gas, more coffee, and a chance to stretch out a stiff back.

Fifteen minutes later I was done. Full tank, loosened joints, and a cup of coffee from the station's self-serve snack counter. Well, what doesn't kill ya makes ya stronger, right? Guess I'd find out.

More farmland. More miles. Hey, look, cows! Moving on never seemed so tedious.

Ninety minutes later the farmland started to give way to a handful of tired industrial buildings surrounded not by tractors and combines but by equally tired old sedans and minivans. I was nearing St. Louis, and these were the poor Illinois communities that tried, in vain, to be part of the city but by water and attitude were prevented. I was almost feeling sad for those that lived down here when my cell phone rang. I looked down: Dan.

"Hey, where you at?" he asked, his voice tinny over the phone's speaker.

"The depressing suburbs just before hitting St. Louis. What's up?"

"Just wanting to check in, see how you are after last night," he replied. "Wanted to see if you changed your mind, or if you were on the road, but it sounds like road it is."

"Yeah, I got up and out early," I said, "wanted to try to beat some traffic. Almost worked."

"Just wait, you'll miss that traffic."

"Not a chance in hell."

"So," he continued, "Last night go okay for you?"

"Yeah," I said, "It was fine. Not too much drama, good seeing everyone, it all worked fine. And I didn't get drunk or anything, so I'm good to drive today."

"Always helps. All good with Elena?"

"She was down about it all, but ya kinda expect that," I said. "I mean, I know with the history we have, and the history we don't have but really could've had, I knew she'd be bummed. Heck, I'm bummed, and part of it's because we never did end up doing anything."

"She had plenty of others, pretty much everyone except you and me."

"Oh come on, she's not that bad, but yeah, sometimes I wonder if I should've when the chance was there."

Dan laughed. "Dude, your chance was always there, more than anyone else I know. Hell, it's probably still there, if you turn around and hurry back she'll probably welcome you home with open arms and open legs."

"Yeah, well . . ." I paused and let out a deep sigh, "the moment, as they say, has passed."

"And you'll be back," Dan said, "at least at some point you'll be back, for a little bit or something. Not like you'll never come back to Chicago and see your mom or anything."

"Well yeah, of course I'll come back, not sure when, but I'll . . . I mean, it's not like I'll never ever be back to Chicago again. It just won't be 'me being here', it'll be me blowing through town and maybe or maybe not having time to see everyone again, and that's what's tough, fitting what used to be existence into a particular Friday or Saturday night before I fly home, gosh, hope you're free that night, if not oh well see ya next time I'm in town."

"Well I'd hope you plan on staying in town longer than one night."

"Sure, but family and all."

"Hey, gotta do what ya gotta," Dan said, as if putting an end to any further expectations from anyone regarding my Midwestern availability. "Anyway, all else okay? I know Claire and Gary were kinda bummed too about you takin' off. You know, bummed both because you were leaving, and bummed because they won't be working with you anymore. So just overall bummed, I'd say."

"Yeah, heard a lot of that last night, people happy for me but sad for themselves. A lot of people just happy that I have the whole Sarah thing behind me."

"And that's Elena again," Dan chimed in. "She never liked Sarah."

"Sarah wasn't 'one of us' and never hid the fact that she wasn't and never wanted to be, and when you don't even try to get along, well, . . ."

"Chapter closed, next."

"Yup," I agreed. "So how are you today, you survive last night in one piece?"

"Best I can," he said. "Left probably 5 minutes after you did. A few people were still there, but no reason for me to stay."

"Don't blame ya, long night," I said, "plus, since you set it all up, and thank you for that, I do appreciate it, you were first one there and all, so no need to be last one out."

"Right."

"So at work?"

"Yeah, but taking a break to see how you are and where you are," Dan replied. "But it sounds like all is good, and our intrepid traveler is on his way."

"Best I can. Out of state in mere moments."

"Well, glad you're good, glad traveling is good so far, . . . and thanks for letting me throw you the going away bash last night, I think it was good for everyone, especially you."

"Hey thank you for doing it," I said. "I owe ya."

"Yeah, when you come back to town, golf and dinner are on you."

"Or when you come down to Arizona, it'll be on me then too."

"Sounds like a plan."

"Alrightythen," I said, "I'm gonna drive, and hope to get to my cousin's place by dinner."

"Cool. Drive safe."

"Will do. Talk to ya later."

"You bet," Dan replied, and then the call clicked off.

Five minutes later, there was a wide expanse of cloudy, impatient water directly below my car, and looking left and right I could see it coil into the distance, the shine of the mid-day sun reflecting off the Mississippi River like the bright beckoning glare of a lighthouse directing one home through the fog. I readjusted in my seat and settled in for a long drive west, nodding in acknowledgment to the sunshine that was welcoming me to my new life, even though I wasn't quite there yet.

The early afternoon passed with little trouble or fanfare. Navigating St. Louis' expressways was frustrating – I can't imagine doing so in rush hour every day – but I found my way to 44 West, and watched as the city turned country. Once I was free from the west side, I found myself in a land of hills, small roadside shops hawking antiques of all kinds, and wineries. Dozens of wineries. Who knew central Missouri was a hotbed of winemaking? The scenery, along with the gently undulating ups and downs and slow curves of the highway, had a tranquilizing effect, and by mid-afternoon I was more than ready to reach my evening's destination, the "other Springfield:" Springfield, Missouri, home of my cousin Tim, who was graciously letting me spend the night on his sofa. I hadn't seen Tim in about 3 years, so I was excited about us catching up. Plus, it would be a good night off from thinking about either the past or the future.

By about 4:30 I was passing signs proclaiming that I was now in Springfield, and imploring me to enjoy my stay. I nodded my unspoken assent, and vowed to find enjoyment wherever I could. I started watching for my exit, which my GPS helpfully pointed out was only ¾ of a mile away. I also figured it was time to let Tim know I was close, so I clicked my cell alive, and voice-dialed his number. He answered after 3 rings.

"Hey, Tim, it's Wade, how ya doing?"

"Hey, Wade, great, all good. What's up, you're not canceling your trip are you?"

"No, no," I said, "Hell, I'm almost there now, probably five, ten minutes from your place."

He didn't reply immediately, and there was a bit a dead air before he said, "You're five minutes away now? Today?"

"Yeah, I . . ."

"Oh man, damn it, I'm sorry, I think I screwed up, I thought you were coming through town next week. I'm in Kansas City until Sunday afternoon, I'm not there."

"Oh. Okay, well, no problem, I can . . ."

He cut me off. "No, not to worry, my place is empty and I keep an emergency key around back. Go there, grab the key from under the mat that's under the big barbeque smoker, and go ahead and help yourself to the place. Mi casa, su casa."

"You sure? I mean, I can find a hotel . . ."

"No, no, my fuck-up, you stay at my place."

"You sure?"

"I insist."

"Okay then," I said. "Will do. Anything I should know about your place, your neighbors? Any crazy cat ladies that watch over your block and will call the cops on me for being there?"

He laughed. "No man, you're good, everyone there's cool. And there's a great sports bar barbeque place about 2 blocks away, my neighbor manages it, and the food's great, go there and tell him you're my cousin."

"Will do. Hey, sorry I'm going to miss you."

"Me too, Wade. Been too long. How's Aunt Grace?" My mom.

"Doing okay. Sad that I'm heading out of town, but I promised to call every week, so she's fine. Plus with my sister Beth still there, at least both her kids haven't moved away. Oh, and Beth says hi."

"Tell her hi back," he replied. "Listen, gotta run, but call if you need anything, okay?"

"Will do Tim. Thanks again, I appreciate this."

"No sweat cuz. Talk to ya later."

Welcome to Springfield, Missouri. Now what?

I made my way to Tim's house, parked in the driveway, and found the key with little effort. Once inside, I turned on a few lights, gave myself a quick tour of the house, made an executive decision that the extra bedroom would suit me just fine for the night, and then dropped my bag on the floor and flopped on the bed. A dog barked in the distance. Then he stopped, and the quiet lulled me to sleep.

I rolled over in an unfamiliar room in the dark about an hour and a half later. I grabbed my phone off the night table; 6:42. Okay, so that explains why my stomach is growling. I lay there for a moment before getting up; it was quiet, peaceful. No expectations or agendas. No place I needed to be, no one waiting for me. No "usual place" to go to, with the usual faces and sounds and smells. It was . . . . different. Nice. Relaxing. Also uneasy, as if something were wrong, as if I was doing something wrong, and the other shoe was about to fall.

Nah. Stop thinking.

Now about food – oh, yeah, the local BBQ joint. I got out of bed, grabbed a jacket and my keys, and made my way to the car. While walking, I opened my Google Maps app on my phone, and it zeroed in on where I was. I zoomed in to see the immediate area around me, and there it was, 2 blocks south and another block west: Big Bear BBQ. Must be the place. Fantastic. Next stop: Big Bear BBQ.

The place was just as one would expect for a college town sports bar-barbeque joint. I pulled into the parking lot, which was a half-full mixture of pickup trucks, import luxury cars, SUVs, and rusted wrecks. The place itself was a free-standing wooden building, reminiscent of an abandon Cracker Barrel, only older and with none of the kitsch and plenty of hickory smoke permeating the air. I walked up to the front-and-center door, pushed it open, and stepped in.

It was a noisy Friday night crowd, the mix of people almost perfectly aligning with the mix of vehicles out front. Indeed, it wouldn't make for a very challenging game to play "Match the Patron with their Vehicle." I nodded to the lithe sorority girl at the front counter, pointed toward the back wall, and headed toward the sprawling bar at the rear of the room. "Sprawling" doesn't do it justice: it seemed to start somewhere near St. Louis, and appeared to end near Tulsa. Which was fine with me, since that meant plenty of seating options where I wouldn't be mashed between sweaty, large men or groups over-served frat boys. I weaved my way between the crowded tables and found an empty seat near the center of the bar, a large-screen TV facing me broadcasting two colorfully outfitted football teams.

Within moments the bartender approached. She was probably within a year or two of my age, an attractive brunette with should length hair, and she wore jeans along with a simple black t-shirt with the Big Bear BBQ logo splashed across the front. She wore her smile easily, and greeted me with a friendly "Hi there" as if we were old pals.

25

"What would you like?" she asked.

"Sam Adams on tap?"

"You got it," she replied, and stepped away. Moments later a tall glass filled with amber heaven was placed in front of me. "Menu?"

"Sure," I said. "Oh, and by the way, my cousin said I should come here and say hello for him."

"Who's your cousin?"

"Tim Lippert."

Her smile widened. "Oh my God, you're Tim's cousin? That's so cool. Hi, I'm Amy." She placed a menu on the bar and extended her hand.

I reached over that bar and shook her hand. "Hi Amy, I'm Wade. Tim told me this was the place to come for barbeque while I'm in town, so here I am."

"Nice to meet you, Wade. I'm glad Tim told you to come in. Where is he, is he going to be meeting you here?"

"Unfortunately no," I said, "I thought he'd be in town right now, I'm just passing through on my way west and stopped in to see him, but he's out of town so I'm crashing at his place for the night. Just bad timing all the way around."

"Well that's too bad," she said, "but at least you're here. And I'm glad he told you to come here, he's such a good guy."

"He is," I agreed. I glanced at the menu. "So, what's the best here, what should I get?"

"It's Missouri," she chuckled, "you get baby back ribs or pulled pork, and ours are the best around."

"There ya go then," I said, "pulled pork sandwich and a side of fries."

She grabbed the menu and smiled. "Excellent choice," she said, and stepped away to put in the order.

I took a long pull of the beer, then payed a bit of attention to the TV behind the bar. Not exactly sure who was playing, but the team in black and neon yellow was beating the heck out of the team with white jerseys and navy pants, and that seemed to be upsetting a few guys down the bar watching in earnest. I looked around; families, groups of guys in their twenties who looked like local college kids, a few construction worker types with heavy boots and flannel shirts, a sprinkling of females (some alone at the bar, others in groups), even a young guy and girl at the far end of the bar in full black goth garb. Yeah, this place must have damn good barbeque if it fits for all those disparate customer profiles.

Amy made her way back toward me, then leaned on the bar. "Be a few more minutes on the pork," she said. "Not in a hurry, are ya?"

"Nope," I replied, "none at all. Plan to sit here for a while, have a few drinks, eat barbeque, and talk to you whenever you come by. That's my evening."

She smiled. "That works." She pointed at my beer. "Another?"

"Not yet," I said. "Pacing myself."

She smiled. "Great, just means you'll be here longer." Someone called her name, and she walked off to take care of whatever the issue was — probably more beer needed by someone. The job, right?

Five minutes later Amy reappeared carrying a plate artfully topped by a huge pulled pork sandwich with a small mountain of fries ringing it. She placed it carefully in front of me, then set down the usual napkin-wrapped utensils. "Enjoy," she said. "'Nother beer now?"

"That would be perfect," I said. "Thanks."

"You bet." She turned again toward the taps, while I wrestled with impure thoughts about the food in front of me. Food porn, I think it's called. Either way . . .

Twenty minutes later it was nothing more than a pleasant memory. Better than pleasant, actually, it was damn near the best barbeque I'd ever had. I must've been sitting there with an expression that echoed that thought, because Amy came back and said with a smile, "That good, huh?"

"Good lord yes," I said. "That was seriously, seriously great. Good recommendation."

"Owner's been a pitmaster for about 35 years, one of the best in this part of the country. Won awards and competitions and everything." She pointed to the far side wall, and I saw the large glass case that held dozens of large silver and gold trophies, many topped by small pigs. Yup, the pitmaster knew what the hell he was doing.

"Not surprised. That was phenomenal."

"Glad to hear it," she said as she picked up my plate and carried it away.

I spent the next hour or so nursing another beer along with a glass of water, just watching the people, the TV, generally enjoying the solitude of companionship that one gets as an invisible member of a larger crowd. No great agendas, no deep thoughts — just me and a bar and bar patrons. And thanks to the generous size of the bar itself, never did anyone sit on either of the stools next to me, affording me the space I was wanting that evening. I made a mental note to send Tim not only a thank you card for this recommendation, but maybe an Amazon gift card as well. This was just what I needed.

Eventually as the dinner crowd cleared out and the restaurant slowed a bit, Amy returned. She leaned on the bar, chin cupped in both hands. "So, you said you were heading west. What brings you out there that requires driving instead of flying?" When I didn't immediately answer, she said, "Or am I asking things that I shouldn't be asking?"

"No, no, it's fine," I said. "Just thinking about the wording of it all."

"Ooh, a story," she said, "this sounds good." She grabbed a stool that was behind the bar and pulled it close so she could sit on it. "Okay, so tell me your story."

So for the next ten minutes I provided an abbreviated version of the story, from the marriage breakdown, through divorce, and ending where I sat, at the end of day one of my trek from old home to new home. She sat attentive and listened, nodding where appropriate, and when I finished and paused, she sat back, tilted her head, and looked at me. She didn't say anything right away, so I took a sip, looked back at her, and shrugged.

"I'm afraid to ask what you're thinking," I said. "Either I'm an idiot, or I'm crazy, right?"

"No, nothing like that," she replied. "Just thinking that, well, on one hand, it takes guts to pull up and leave like that, no matter the situation. On the other hand, some people might look at it as trying to run from life's troubles, and God knows you can't run from life."

"Which camp do you fall into, the one hand, or the other?"

"I've never been married and never been divorced, so I have no idea what it might be like to have that happen and feel the need to start over again, so really? I think you might be a bit of both. But what do I know."

"You're not the first person to think that," I said. "Hell, just last night, going away gathering of some of my friends, and I had more than one person tell me I was crazy for moving away. Actually, one of them used a lot more colorful way of saying it, so . . ."

"But I imagine you gotta do what's right for you, right? I mean, nobody can actually be in your shoes except you, so you gotta live your life the way you see fit, and then hope and pray that your decisions work out, and then go from there."

I nodded. "That's about it, that's where I am, and that's all I can hope for."

"Well," she said, "I wish you luck, and I'm glad you passed through here. So tell me, why Sedona? You know people there, or have family there?"

"I'm told Sedona is a Hopi word for 'peace,' which sounded perfect for what I need right now," I replied. "Just need a little peace, and little time, and place to recharge and then begin again."

"No family or anything?"

"I had an uncle in Winslow, Arizona for a long time, but he moved about seven years ago. And besides, Winslow's in a different part of the state." I paused. "No, I've just seen enough about Sedona, pictures and all, and heard so much about the place, about the spiritual vibe, the pace of life, how the people go about their lives, it just seemed like the right place for me. It's just sort of calling me, so I'm answering."

"Works for me," she said. "And you're coming from Chicago, were you born there? Is that your original home?"

"Yeah. Well, suburbs, actually, but saying Chicago, everybody knows what and where Chicago is."

"I've been there a few times over the years," she said, "I had a cousin who lived outside of Chicago, so I visited her bunch of times when we were young, but I didn't actually get into Chicago, I don't think. Most often her family came out here in the summer, and we'd all meet at the Ozarks and spend a few weeks together."

"Where was your cousin from?"

"Oh geez, some little town west of Chicago . . . . what was it? Hmmm . . . ." She pursed her lips in thought. "Damn, something with a 'G' but I can't remember it . . ."

"Glenview," I asked? When she shook her head no, I continued, "Glen Ellyn?"

"Nope."

"Well, I grew up in a far west town, Geneva, . . ."

She looked up. "Ohmygod, that's it, Geneva Illinois, that's where Natalie grew up. You can't be serious, you're from there too? How crazy is that."

I stopped and stared. "Natalie? Natalie what?"

"Natalie Salerno, why?"

I let the name, Natalie Salerno, echo through my head for a moment, let it bounce off dusty memories and key old sepia-toned images. "No . . . fucking . . . way . . ." I slowly said. "No, you're kidding me, right? Natalie Salerno? Natalie Salerno is your cousin?"

"You knew her?" Amy looked wide-eyed, and sat up straight? "Wait, you knew . . . holy shit. No way . . . . holy shit. You're Wade . . . I mean, you're THAT Wade . . . that's you?"

"If we're on the same page here, which I think we are, then yes, I'm that Wade, as in 'her boyfriend during her junior year of high school' Wade, as in 'took her to prom' Wade, yes, that's me." I sat back, almost fell of the stool, and then regained my balance and composure. "There's no way . . . I mean, . . . of all the gin joints in all the world, and all . . . I cannot believe you're Natalie's cousin. This is crazy."

She sat back on her stool behind the bar. "Wow, this is, . . . this is so weird."

I continued. "Yeah, I was a year older than Nat, and after I graduated we broke up, then I went away to college, and you know, like teenagers do we drifted our separate ways and we never did keep in touch. And now, I'm probably one of the last people on earth not on Facebook, so I'm really out-of-touch on where people have gone and what they've done. So what's she doing now, where is she?" I paused. "I mean, I'd love to drop her a line and say hello, provided she'd want to hear form me." I paused again until the silence was awkward, then continued. "I mean, you know, if she'd want to hear from me. I know when we broke up she took it kinda hard . . . we both did, and I always . . ." I stopped.

Amy was silent, staring down toward the bar. I leaned toward her, and peered up at her. "You okay? Something wrong?"

She slowly looked up. "You don't know."

"Don't know what?"

"Natalie died a little over two years ago."

I looked back at Amy. "What the hell . . . Natalie died? Nat's . . . . she's dead?"

"I thought you would've heard."

"What, how? What happened?"

"Ovarian cancer. She was only 33. It was, well, it was rather sudden, she had some things that weren't right, went to the doctor, had tests, and they said she had cancer, and then about seven months later she was gone. That quick." Amy's eyes were tearing as she spoke, and she wiped at her right eye with the side of her hand as she spoke. "She wasn't married, she'd moved to Oklahoma City for work and had been living there for a while, so when she got sick she came up here and moved in with me and my mom, and we helped take care of her. And then her mom moved down here for a while as well, to be close to her for as long as possible."

"Wow." I was shaking my head ever so slightly. "I'm so, so sorry, . . . I wish I had known, I've really not stayed in touch with people from high school, so I had no idea." I reached over and put my hand on hers. "I'm so sorry for you, not only losing a cousin, but being there and seeing it happen, God, I'm so sorry."

"No," she wiped away another tear, "it's fine, thanks, but I got to spend time with her, as much time as possible, so there's that, which was good. Plus, it really brought us closer together, which I think we both loved, and I know I'll cherish forever, so that came out of it as well."

Natalie had been my first love, and it was impossible for me to think about my senior year in high school without thinking of her, and remembering all of the things we did together. She was the first person I can ever remember telling me that she believed in me, that I was special, and I remember holding her and thinking that as long as I had her in my arms I was special. So many simple, singular moments of Natalie came flooding back in rapid fire: her coming up behind me at my locker and tickling me; walking home from school one day when it started raining, and we ran and hid under the eaves of a liquor store sign and got dirty looks from a few of the customers there; Homecoming dance, her in a gorgeous midnight blue dress, me feeling like the luckiest person in the school; driving her home after a basketball game, and she spilled a milkshake all over both of us, and we laughed and laughed.

The first time, for both of us, in her bedroom one afternoon after school when her parents were at work and her sister was on a late field trip, and how Natalie looked and smelled and felt, and how afterward she smiled and looked at me and told me it was a perfect afternoon.

And that August evening, maybe seven weeks after I graduated, when we were both in tears, both of us knowing I'd be leaving soon and life for us both would change and it would be best to not let things linger, that it would be best to break up now and see what happened over the next year and maybe see where we both were next June, when she graduated. She said a long-distance relationship would work, that my school in Ohio was only five hours away, and I'd come home for weekends once a month, and she'd come visit, and we'd talk on the phone, and damn-it it would work. I told her that having a boyfriend 300 miles away was no way to celebrate senior year in high school, that she should be having fun then and there, not thinking about the occasional weekend while her friends were going to football games and parties and plays and dances. She said she couldn't imagine school without me, and that she hated me. And that she loved me. And like that, it was over.

We crossed paths a few times over the next year. The last time I ever saw her or spoke to her was about a year after we broke up. We were both at the same party, late July just before she left for her freshman orientation at University of Colorado, and we said hi, talked about what I was doing, about how excited she was to get away from home . . . and then we drifted off to separate conversations in other parts of the house, and that was it. I never saw her again. Didn't stop me from thinking about her on and off the next few years, but as the years passed her face invaded my dreams with less frequency. Whenever I did think about her it was with tremendous warmth and affection, and hopes that she was safe and happy and successful. Life goes on.

And for Natalie, it did, right up until it didn't.

"I haven't seen her or talked to her in years. I mean, you know, it's been a long, long time, life moved in a different direction, I got married, got older, and she sort of just became that high school girlfriend that you think about every now and then, when the topic of high school comes up. Really, I haven't thought much about her, about us, in a while." I stopped, shook my head, took a breath. "But I suddenly miss her very, very much right now" I said. "It just never occurred to me that somehow, somewhere, I wouldn't see her again. It doesn't seem real."

Amy came around the bar and wrapped her arms around me, giving me a deep, warm hug. Neither of us said anything, and I turned and put my arms around her as well. We remained there, holding on, not wanting to let go.

Once we let go, Amy said, "Are you okay? This probably wasn't what you were expecting from this night."

"Yeah, I'll be okay. It's sudden, hearing this about someone from the long-ago, someone you used to be so close to, but ya know, like I said, it's not like we've had any relationship for the past 15 years or so. I mean, it's sad, really damn sad, more for you than me I'm sure, but it's not devastating, just sad." I grabbed her hands. "Leaving for college, breaking up with her then, now that was devastating. This is out of left field, if you know what I mean." She nodded, and I continued. "This sucks on a lot of levels. Thirty, thirty-one, that's too young to die, it's too soon for someone who I remember being so young and full of life. Having your whole life ahead of you, that's just, just, . . ." I shook my head and let me words trail off.

"Can I get you another drink, another beer?"

"No, I said, "I should probably go back to Tim's place, just take this all in, get some sleep," I said, and I embraced her again. "You have things to do, and I need to keep going, I'll, . . . I'll be fine."

"Listen," she said, "hold on." She scurried back around the bar, grabbed a business card and pen, and scribbled something on the back. Then she walked to me and handed it to me. "My number's on back, I'm off at 11:00. If you want to talk, call, okay?"

"Thanks, okay."

"No, Wade, I mean it, if you need anything, have any questions, anything, I'm only a few blocks from Tim's place, you call me, okay?"

"Thanks Amy, I really do appreciate it, I appreciate everything." We hugged again, and I dropped enough cash on the bar to cover the bill and tip. "How about, if I don't call you tonight, I at least call you tomorrow morning before I leave."

"Okay, that'll work. But please, call, I want to hear from you before you go. Promise?"

"Promise." One final hug, and then I turned and walked out.

I sat on the sofa at Tim's place, television off, lights off, nothing but the street light illuminating the room through the half-drawn plantation shutters. I was still trying to wrap my head around the fact that Natalie was gone. And part of that was trying to figure out why it bothered me so much when I hadn't been in contact with her for over fifteen years. Yes, she had, at one time in my life, been perhaps the most important person in my life. And yes, she had played a starring role (probably THE starring role) in my transformation from kid to young adult. But still — that was years ago, a lifetime ago. Why did this feel so heavy, so much like a wave engulfing me, holding me under the surf and not letting me breathe? So I sat on the sofa and let myself relive so many of our moments together, as if keeping her alive in my mind would keep her alive in body as well.

I had been sitting there for a while – I really wasn't paying attention to time – when the doorbell rang. I picked up my phone and clicked it alive: 11:48. Who was Tim expecting at this time of night? As I rose from the couch, my tired mind started racing toward other, more nefarious reasons for the late night visitor. Was Tim a drug dealer? Jealous ex? Angry bookie? I walked to the door and peered out the hole.

Amy.

I opened the door. "Hey there," I said.

"You still up? Did I wake you," she asked. "I didn't see any lights on, but thought I'd risk trying."

"Nope, still up," I said, "just sitting, digesting the evening. C'mon in." I stepped back and held the door, and she passed into the living room. She had a small book with her, which she placed on the coffee table as she took off her leather jacket. "Please, have a seat," I said, motioning to the sofa. As she sat I switched on the old wooden lamp that sat on the end table. The glow was startling, and it took my eyes a few moments to adjust.

"So, ... hi again," I said. "What's up?"

"Well, when I was thinking about tonight and about Natalie, I remembered something, so I went home after work and checked it out, and it was what I thought it was, so I wanted to let you know and let you see it." She reached to the table and grabbed the book, and I sat down next to her on the sofa.

"This is – was – Natalie's diary, or journal, whatever you want to call it," Amy said. "She was never a big diary person, but when she got sick she started writing in it a lot. And, . . ." Amy opened the diary to the last page, where four envelopes were neatly tucked into the flap. She thumbed through them, then pulled one of them out and handed it to me. Neatly handwritten on the front was *Wade Benthagen*. Me. My name.

"Before she died, Natalie wrote a few letters, she said they were her closure with some of the people in her life, over her life, that had meant a lot to her, or the most to her. And I was thinking that one of them was to you, so I went home and dug this out and checked , . . ."

"And one was for me."

"Yeah."

"Sooooo . . . ." I held the envelope in my hand, turned it over then turned it back to the writing, "Do I read it now, or later, or do you want me to read it now so you can have it back, or . . ."

She shook her head. "I don't know, you're the first person I've gotten one of these to," she said. "This is new to me."

We both sat back. I held the envelope up, as if I was looking through it, then brought it back to my lap and turned to look at her. "This is going to open a lot of memories and hurt like hell, isn't it?"

"I have no idea what she wrote," Amy said. "Natalie just wrote these and told me that if I ever happen to come across any of these people, there were letters. That's all she said."

"Ya know, I'm just not sure I want to read this right now," I said, dropping the envelope on the table. "I mean, I do want to read it, just, . . . just not yet. Not now. Not tonight."

Amy nodded. "Yeah, I get it," she said, "when you're ready it'll be there."

"Thanks," I replied. "Right now, I just wanna let my mind go, let the image of Nat go, and just fall asleep. I just don't wanna think about it. I don't wanna . . . I need time to adjust to this, to accept that she's gone." I sprawled back on the sofa and closed my eyes. "This was not what I planned for my first night on the road." Perhaps ten seconds later Amy leaned over, her head nestling on my shoulder.

"Nobody can plan for something like this," she said. "All we can do is hold on to someone and get through it."

I brought my hand down around her shoulder, and she burrowed into my side. We sat there, curled into each other, until silently we each fell asleep.

Brian C. Holmsten

Saturday, October 18

When I awoke I was curled up in Amy's arms. She, too, was sleeping. The soft light from the table lamp was fighting for attention with the sunshine that was beginning to leak through the shutters. I uncoiled myself, which jostled Amy, which led to both of us slowly stretching, sitting up, trying to work the kinks out of our backs and legs and shoulders from a night of intertwined sleep on the couch. I sat up, removed my glasses, rubbed my eyes. She stood and stretched skyward. Then she turned toward me.

"You okay?"

"I think so," I said. "Life feels a little different this morning, a little off kilter."

"Well sure," she said. "It was a big jump from 'haven't thought of her for years' to 'thinking about her being gone now.' Not the normal stuff that happens in any given day."

She leaned over to pick up the letter that was lying on the table. She held it out to me. "Don't lose this."

I reached for it, then stopped. She shrugged, then held it out again with a bit of a shake. I leaned over and gently took it from her hand. "Thanks." I stood. "So like, you're not married, are you? I mean, is there a pissed off husband looking for you, and I'm gonna be in the wrong place here?"

She laughed. "No, nobody will be comin' through the door with guns blazing, you're safe."

"Okay, well, that's good," I said, "because that would really be the icing on the cake here." I looked at her for a moment, then continued. "One more thing, if I might ask."

"Anything."

"When Natalie died, what happened to her?" She pursed her lips and cocked her head like a confused spaniel. "I mean, was there a funeral, was she buried, ..."

"Oh, oh, okay," she replied, "Yeah, uhm, there was a funeral for her, then she was buried in a small cemetery up in Camdenton, that's a town near Lake of the Ozarks where we always summered. She loved that area, so Natalie and her family decided it would be appropriate. It's a little over an hour away, but it's going northeast, the wrong direction for you, so . . ."

"Right," I said, "But I'd kinda like to go and say goodbye, I'm this close, who knows when I'll ever get back through here again."

"Sure, I completely get it. I can text you the name and address of it, but . . . ." She hesitated.

"But what?"

She took a breath. "Listen, I just think, maybe it would be better if you had some company. I mean, I know where it is, I could go with you, get you there, you'd have someone to talk to, that sort of thing." When I didn't say anything she continued. "And it's not an inconvenience for me, you'll need to come back through town anyway, so you can drop me back off. And right now, I'd just rather not see you drive off alone to do this."

"I . . . . I appreciate it," I said slowly. "I may not be very good company, I may not be talkative, . . ."

"No, I get it, sure, but at least you'd have someone with you, and I think that would be good."

"You sure I'm not wrecking your day? I mean, I can do this myself, I'm a big boy, I made it here on my own."

She stepped to me and put her arms around me, giving me a deep hug. "I know. But you don't have to do everything alone, especially the tough stuff." She pulled back. "Not stuff like this."

"Well then, that would be good, I'd appreciate it," I said. "Do you need to get home, shower, whatever, before we leave?"

"Give me ten, fifteen minutes, and I'll be back here and we can go."

"Okay, works for me. See you in a bit."

She nodded, smiled, and hurried out the front door.

I quickly showered, dressed in clean clothes, packed my bag, and let myself out. I locked the door, replaced the key under the grill, and threw my bag into the trunk of the car. As I was closing the trunk, Amy drove up.

"You ready?"

"As much as I'm gonna be without coffee," I replied, and opened the passenger door for her. She slid in; I closed the door, and made my way around, and jumped in behind the wheel.

"There's a Starbucks drive-thru just before the expressway, how about we hit that first?" she said.

"Perfect," I said. Five minutes later we had coffee in our hands and were on the expressway, headed north toward Camdenton.

After a few silent minutes, Amy broke spoke up. "So, whatcha thinking?"

"I'm not sure," I said. "This seems a bit like I'm watching me outside myself . . . like I'm watching myself on TV, and I'm not really part of what's going on, if that makes sense. I feel foggy, distant, and a little bit like this isn't real, like I'm having a crazy real dream." I looked toward her. "Does that make sense?"

"Yeah, I think so," she replied. "Think about it; what, 12 hours ago, this news was dropped on you. Now, here you are, middle of reinventing yourself and you're going in the wrong direction, heading to find someone to say goodbye, someone who you never thought you'd be saying goodbye to. Foggy and disassociated doesn't begin to describe how I'd be feeling if it was me."

"And ya know," I said, "it's not even so much the goodbye, it's, . . . it's, . . . hell, I'm not even sure what it is, what I'm doing this for. It's just, I need to do this. I have to do it. I can't leave here without seeing her one last time. I really can't explain it, not right now, but I just need to do this." I picked up my coffee and took a quick sip. "And I have no idea what to expect there, what I'll do, I, . . . I just, . . ." I took another sip. "It's the Indiana Jones thing, I'm making this up as I go along."

"Makes sense to me," she said. "Not like you ever can plan for this stuff, even when you see it happening in front of you."

"God yeah, that's right," I said, "you were with her when it all happened, weren't you? Jeez, that had to have been tough, seeing her as the cancer took over, . . . was it difficult? I mean, for you? I know it must've been hell for her, but, . . ."

"It was the most helpless feeling I've ever had in my life." Her turn to take a sip of coffee. "You want to help, you want to do something . . .

anything, any damn thing, and you can't, you, . . . you can do things but none of it matters, none of it helps, and no matter what you do life doesn't go back to how it was.

"I mean, there were times when I'd be with her, and she'd be so damn sick, and it just broke my heart seeing her like that, and then the next day she'd be like a different person, she'd be so much better it would be like she was barely sick, and I'd think 'This is great, she's beating it, she's gonna make it,' and then a day later, back to being so sick again, . . . and at times like that, you start having no idea what to do, what helps, what makes anything better, and then you just get so damn upset and sad, . . ."

I nodded. "And then I would imagine you get frustrated with yourself, because you're supposed to be supporting her, and here you are feeling bad and helpless and weak."

"Oh my God, you have no idea," she said, "and then guilt, and then you try to carry the whole burden for her, and then, . . ." She slowly sipped her coffee. I caught a quick glance, and she had tears in her eyes. "And then she's gone, and there was never anything you could've done, and all that's left is a void."

"And memories," I said, "you'll always have those."

"Yeah, sure, and sometimes those are great, and sometimes it feels empty and incomplete."

"Incomplete. Yeah, that, . . . I know that feeling, that's I think where I am now," I said. "When we broke up, it was so hard on both of us, and then time passed, and we both moved on, life an all, . . . but it's funny, I thought of her a few times recently, the past few years, probably because I was in the middle of another relationship ending, an' I wondered how she was, all that, . . . and I always thought someday, maybe at a school reunion or something, that we'd be able to say hi again, talk, just make things right on how it all ended. You know?"

"Closure, sure."

"Yeah, closure, but I also think, . . . I guess I had always hoped that any pain that was left, any bad feelings that might have lingered, those could be put to rest and be wiped clean, ya know? Kinda, . . ."

"I don't think there was ever any pain left, not by this time," Amy said. "Nat never talked about any pain or hurt when she mentioned you, or high school, or any of her relationships." She sipped her coffee, and turned toward me. "She was I think a lot stronger and forgiving than you give her credit for. She was hurt, made peace with it, and moved on.

40

That's what you do." She put her hand on my arm and gave it a couple of quick pats. "You should try it sometime."

"Yeah, well . . . gettin' there. I'm working on that with the ex-wife and how that played out as well, so . . ."

"One step at a time," she said, "get through today, this morning, and go from there."

We were quiet for a few minutes, then I said, "Thank you for coming up here with me today. This, . . . well, I'm not sure it really makes it easier, but in a way, . . ."

"No, I get it, and you're welcome. Again, looking at the big mystical picture here, I think this, us, this was all supposed to happen. And I really wouldn't have felt right about sending you up here on your own, dealing with all this, all these emotions, on your own."

"I've dealt with emotions before."

"You know what I mean," she said, "Don't be an island, let people in to help every now and then. Me wanting to come up here with you doesn't mean you're weak, it means I want to help and offer support. Doesn't mean I don't think you can do it, . . . just means you can do it better with someone."

"Well, thank you."

"Okay," she said, "Next exit, get off here and then take a left." When the exit came up I eased off, stopped at the sign, then turned left. Halfway there.

The next 30 minutes we drove through some of the most beautiful scenery I had ever seen. Though it was mid-October, the trees were in full color, with vivid reds, oranges and yellows along both sides of the road, hanging like bunting from New York skyscrapers during a parade. The air was cool, a comforting contrast to the warmth of the sun as it shone through the car glass. Neither of us said much, other than commenting on the scenery or a quick "you doing okay?" We passed barns that resembled replicas from my childhood train set, and farms replete with cattle, pigs, chickens, goats, and even a few llamas. I slowed for the occasional tractor pulling hay or corn, and crawled through the tiny towns that dotted the route every ten minutes and looked as though they were Rockwell paintings come alive. Eventually I saw the tired sign, almost hidden by a vibrant red ash: "Welcome to Camdenton, Gateway to Ozarks Country."

"Camdenton, this is it, right?" I said.

"Yeah, in about a half a mile we need to turn right at the church, you can't miss it, a perfect little white church with an odd blue steeple." She turned toward me. "That's where the funeral service was, then the cemetery is just down the road."

I slowed and watched for the white church with a blue steeple that would mark my turn. Within two blocks I saw it, standing guard over a small garden. I made my turn, and carefully drove down the worn road that turned from cracked blacktop to dirt in a half mile. Ahead, on the left, I saw the stone gates with the iron transom overhead. Camdenton Prairie Cemetery. This was it. I pulled in, then paused. "Where now?"

"Follow to the right."

I slowly followed the drive to the right at the split. "Okay, now look for a bronze fountain," she said. I saw the fountain after maybe 50 yards. I stopped the car and cut the engine, and we stepped out. "Over to the left, past the fountain," Amy said.

I was striking how quiet and silent it was. No traffic, no cars, no farm machinery, not even any birds nesting in nearby trees. No sound at all except for a slight breeze that tickled my ears and gently caressed the random flower arrangements adorning two or three grave sites. I walked gingerly over the ground, passed the fountain, and then began to slowly scan headstones, looking for the familiar name. The fourth one I came to, brown marble with crisp white lettering, was what I was looking for.

It was elegant, simple, and bittersweet.

Natalie Elizabeth Salerno. 1980 – 2013.

I stood frozen in place, staring, unable to digest the words and dates I was seeing, wanting almost to look around and see if this was a set-up, a joke, waiting for her to jump out from behind the fountain and yell "Gotcha!" But no, I stood in silence, looking at the stone, the last tangible artifact of Natalie's existence in this world.

Amy put her hand on my shoulder. "I'm going to take a walk, you take all the time you need."

"Mmm-hmm, thanks," I barely said. She walked away, leaving me staring at the headstone, the name, the deep green grass.

And then I felt stupid, thinking that I should have stopped and bought flowers, angry with myself for coming all the way out here and not bringing her anything. For Christ sakes, I hadn't seen her in years and I can't even remember to bring a gift? What the hell's wrong with you, Wade?

And before I could get more annoyed with myself, I took a deep, audible breath, let it out slowly, and knelt in front of the stone, respectfully off to the side. I reached out, touched it; it was hard, cold, smooth. Finite. Only one thing left to do.

"Natalie," I said softly. "My god, Natalie. I . . . I wish . . . I wish you could be here now, so I could talk to you, or so we could have a conversation. We never got that chance again, did we, after you graduated, never got to sit down, reconnect, . . ." I looked up toward the bright blue sky, as if the right words would appear. Then I glanced back at the stone, and lowered myself to sit next to it. This could take a while.

"I miss you Nat, especially today. There have been so many times, . . . life hasn't gone exactly as well as I'd hoped, and there've been times when I wished I could just go back to high school, to being 17 and 18 again, to us, that year, to how we were when we were together, . . . and I think of how happy we were, I know I was, and how incredibly beautiful you were, your smile, your voice, your playfulness, . . . and man, I wish I could live that year over again, do it all the exact same way, feel the same way, . . .

"And, ya know, we went our separate ways, people do that, high school sweethearts do it all the time, . . . and I wondered how you were, where you were, what you were doing, who you were with, . . . and it was never, I never regretted us going our own ways, but I always wondered, what would it have been like if we'd met when we were older, maybe 23 or 24, what would've happened then? Or had both gone to the same college? And, ya know, ya can't change history or anything, but I just wish . . . I just wish we could've had a second shot."

I paused for a second, and spent a few moments grooming the blades of grass at the base of the stone. "I got married, I did become a writer, so that was one thing from high school that came true, of course I'm a marketing and advertising writer, so it's kinda mercenary, but at least I write like I always wanted to. And yeah, I got married, her name's Sarah, but we got divorced a couple years ago, and . . . and it's funny, I'm having a hard time forgiving myself for letting us split apart. Not like I cheated or anything like that, although, well, I could have, . . . and at times I really wanted to . . . . but it was just, our tracks met, then over time the tracks started parting farther and farther away, and we weren't going in the same direction, just different degrees of it, so it really wasn't the same . . . and just, we just grew apart. That's lame, and cliché, but it's what it is. And what's funny, Nat, is I had such a hard time of that when we broke up, and any other relationship, when it ended, I always felt more responsible, and now this with Sarah, it just feels like I gave up, and I feel guilty."

I looked up at her name on the stone. "And I think it hurts because, the truth is, before Sarah, you were the one woman, girl, female, whatever, that I really, really loved. I mean, Nat, you . . . you, I thought you and I . . . . and then when I left for college, and I knew it was somewhere you weren't going to go, I knew it was best for us, . . . I mean, you knew it too, but I think my leaving really forced the hand earlier than you or I wanted, . . . and I've always felt like us ending, and us ending before knowing what might have been, was my fault. And I think I'm feeling the same guilt now, with Sarah, that I did with you, even though it hasn't registered until now."

I paused, picked at more grass. "And then I think, maybe you knew me better than anyone, ever, and that makes me sad, makes me really feel like I fucked up, . . .

"But then, maybe it just wasn't meant to be. Maybe I had to learn these things all by myself. But if it took you dying for me to get it, then it sucks, I would rather have been blissfully unaware and still have you here, and I was never asked about that trade, you for my self-awareness."

I stopped talking, and let the silence creep back into the moment. I looked up, around – nothing, nobody. Just me, alone, with . . . with what, exactly? Stones. Monuments. A bronze fountain.

"Shit. I'm so sorry, Nat. I've always loved you, I hope somewhere, somehow, you know that, or knew that. You're the best thing that ever happened in my life, and I wouldn't be here, who I am, without you, and even though it was a long time ago, . . . just, thank you. Thank you for being you. For loving me, believing in me. And I'll read your letter, promise, when I'm able. When I'm ready. I promise."

I stood up, shook the dust from my jeans. I took out my phone, opened the camera app, and took a picture of the stone, her name. Satisfied that it was good, I clicked the phone off and dropped it back in my pocket.

"I will always love you, Natalie Salerno," I said, and I turned and made my way back to the car, eyes moist. Amy climbed in shortly thereafter, and I leaned toward her and enveloped her in a hug, needing to feel someone. We sat there, arms around each other, for a few minutes.

When I pulled away, she looked into my eyes.

"You okay?"

"No. Maybe. Not sure." I let out a deep breath. "Thank you."

She nodded. I turned the key, fired the engine, and u-turned to get out. I pulled onto the street, and listened, as, for the first time since I had been there, I could hear a sound, that of the church bells jauntily chiming. It was time for something.

Retracing my steps away from Camdenton was done in a bit of a haze, as the roads and sights were familiar but seemed as I was viewing it all through a lens, like I was watching rather than doing. Neither Amy nor I spoke for the first ten minutes, letting the silence cleanse my state of mind. I was almost startled when she said, "So, what are you thinking? Or feeling?"

"Is, is it possible to feel the loss of something you really didn't have?" When she didn't answer, I continued. "I just got divorced, and I'm more sad over this than I am over my divorce, and the divorce was my current life. Shouldn't this be turned the other way around?"

"Didn't you say your divorce was a long time coming, and that you felt like it was over for a while?"

"Yeah, . . . but, . . ."

"But nothing," Amy said, "it sounds, from what you told me, that it was over for you a while back, long before it was 'over over' which gave you a lot of time to deal with it and come to peace with it and file it away under 'closure,' which you never got the chance to do with Natalie." Which made an odd amount of sense. "Seriously," she continued, "you've had other relationships, other girls, women, and those have ended, right? Well, I'd guess nobody just disappeared in the middle of the night, they probably ended with explanations, apologies, whatever, but the fact is they ended, there was closure of some sort. Right?" She looked at me.

"Yeah, right, plenty of relationships, always ended with both sides going different ways, knowing why, so yeah, closure."

"Okay, well you and Natalie kinda ended," and here she used air quotes, "but really you were both so young, it was the first love for both of you, the relationship really wasn't over, it just stopped. You always felt the need to say your piece, apologize, whatever. Now, all this, coming here, it's finally closed. Now you really can move on, start fresh."

"Are you sure you're not some sort of psychologist? Maybe just moonlighting in a bar, picking up stories for a study or something?"

She chuckled. "No, just heard a lot and lived a lot, that's all."

"And what about your living," I said, "if I can get personal for a sec, you said you've never been married, how does that happen to someone as insightful and, well, warm and caring as you, if you'll excuse the odd sideways compliment."

"I've had plenty of relationships, plenty of love and heartbreak, plenty of opportunities for closure, . . ." she paused, and took a deep breath. "But married, well, I'd need to move to a different state for that to happen." I turned to look at her. "And my partner would have to move with me, and she never would. She has a job and parents here in Springfield. So no, not married. But happy."

"You deserve happiness," I said, "and you deserve something very special for spending time with Nat at the end. I'm not sure that's something most people, hell any people, would be comfortable doing." I turned to smile at her. "You're a special person, Amy. Your partner is lucky."

"Thank you for that," she replied. "I keep telling her."

"Keep telling her," I said. "And I hope it's a happiness that lasts forever." I paused, and we drove in silence for a few moments. "Ya know, all this, Natalie, Sarah, you, the reflections, the guilt, the loss, . . . it really makes me wish I had created something with someone that would've lasted forever, ya know? It seems like, when I look back at my life, my love life, that I get happy and then I get unhappy, and nothing lasts. I'd like something to last."

"Isn't that what you're doing, heading out to begin again, start new, re-boot?"

"Yeah, but I've lost time, and . . ."

She shook her head. "No, no, you've got plenty of time left. Every day you're given the chance to create something that lasts forever, whether it's love, work, art, music, whatever. The idea," and she poked my arm, "is to not wait. Don't get lost in what was or what might have been. Get lost in today, and what you can do now."

"Sounds easy."

"It can be if you want it to be."

"So," I asked, "what was Natalie doing, or creating, when all this happened to her? When she thought, . . . I mean, what was she doing with life up til life was interrupted?"

"She was a Special Ed teacher, she taught grade school age kids with learning disabilities."

"Holy smokes," I said, "that's, that's . . . that's so Natalie. She always wanted to do something that meant something, you know, no corporate job, nothing faceless."

"She was great with the kids, too," Amy said. "She came down to Okie City not just because of the position, but because the district was starting up a new program that Nat really believed in, something she actually was involved with in college, something one of her Masters advisors worked on. So she was really into it, and really determined to see it work, not just to see it work but because she really believed it was good for the kids. It really was her passion."

"And she never got married?"

"Close, she was engaged for a bit, but that crashed and burned before the wedding. A few guys, but nothing after Andrew, that was his name, nothing post-Andrew that ever seemed serious."

"That's too bad," I said.

"Shit happens," she said. "Nat was sad for a bit, duh, of course, but she got over it, said it was meant to be and that it freed her up for the 'real' Mr. Right, and she moved on. It never bothered her being single. She wasn't into the whole 'being single' thing, you know, Sex and the City and all, but she was happy with who she was and how her life was playing out."

"Up until . . ."

"Yeah, up until." Amy stretched. "Hey, the expressway is just up ahead."

"Yup, on it," I said, and in a few hundred yards I made my way back onto Route 44, headed back toward Springfield.

Once up to speed in the traffic I continued. "So what else did I miss about Natalie? I feel like I missed out, and now . . ."

"She was probably a lot like you remember," Amy replied. "You knew her when she was becoming herself, that was probably the best, most fun time to have known her."

"Yeah, but I missed out on half of her life. Maybe, if I hadn't . . ."

"Oh fuck, do not go there," Amy said, "no no no, none of this 'if only' bullshit." She turned toward me and leaned closer. "Listen, you two had your time, and it shaped who you both became. And in the case of Nat, that's great, she was a great person, so be happy that you played a part, probably a big part, in her being maybe the best person I ever knew. But do not sit around and wish you had done things differently, 20-20 hindsight is always easy and never realistic. You two had your moment in the sun. When the sun set, you both cried and cursed the darkness, then the sun rose again, whaddaya know about that, and you both had chances to create new moments in the new sun. So do that, for her, okay? Don't mourn what never was. Celebrate the time you two had, and go play in the sun with someone new. Smile a lot, make love a lot, remember her laughter, and be happy that you had what you had. Some people never have even that."

We were both quiet for a mile. I turned toward Amy, and she looked back at me. "So she was really happy?' I said. "She had a good life?"

"Yes, she was happy," Amy replied, "and she was thankful for those in her life, and those who she had touched in life and who had touched her." She leaned over and put an arm around me. "And I know, because she talked about it, that she was thankful for having had you in her life."

I took a breath. "I miss her."

"I miss her too."

Pause. "But I'll move forward."

"We both will. And we'll carry a little bit of her with us."

The next 15 miles passed quickly, and neither of us said anything, content to let the miles and trees and tired barns pass in silence. The Springfield exits were familiar, and I easily navigated back to Tim's place, where her car awaited. We both got out and walked toward her Mini Cooper, the glint of sunshine reflecting off the windshield.

"So," Amy said, "You gonna be okay? No chance on staying another night?"

"Naw," I said, "I'm good. Still in a bit of disbelief, but I can ponder and think while driving as easily as while sitting on Tim's couch."

"If you're sure."

"Yeah, I'm good." We let an awkward beat pass, then I said, "Well, hey, thank you so much . . ."

"Oh, no, really, it was great to meet you," she said, and we embraced in a warm hug. "If you need anything, you still have my card and my number, use it, we're friends now and I'm always there for my friends."

"I appreciate it so, so much," I said, "Thank you for everything, going with me, listening to me, all of it."

48

"She was special to us both."

"She was," I said. "She'd be glad we got to know each other."

"Yeah," Amy said, "I think she's smiling at all this."

One more pause, then I said, "Okay, well, I should hit the road."

"You go, and be careful," Amy said. "Let me know when you land in Sedona, so I know you're okay."

"Will do."

"And Wade?"

"Yeah?"

Amy smiled. "Be good to yourself. You deserve it. Good things are heading to you, just be open to it." And with that she turned and stepped to her car. I watched as she got in, fired the engine and backed out. She waved, smiled, and pulled away.

Time for me to do the same.

I made my way back to Route 44 and re-entered it, this time headed west. The drive was slow, leaving ample time for getting lost in thought. I couldn't shake thoughts of Natalie, my mind flooding with continual images of her, of us, of places form our distant past. I was feeling - what? Emotionally out-of-control? Hmmm . . . mostly it felt as if I were powerless to stop the flow of memories, as if I were simply a passenger, forced to watch, unable to turn off the barrage of mental sights and sounds. My mind was holding me hostage.

I came to this very frightening realization as I drifted out of my lane and almost clipped a semi. I swerved back, shook my head, looked at the speedometer: 84. I looked up: I had no idea where exactly I was, didn't recognize the road. The sign said US 44, but . . .

Even though I had only been driving for 35 minutes, I got off at the next exit, pulled into a gas station, and turned off the car. I sat for a moment, then got out and stepped into the cool air. Thinking that a walk was what I needed to clear my head, I started out down the road, passing the rigs that had stopped for fuel, passing the family haulers that had stopped for Twizzlers and bathroom breaks, and eventually passing the lone McDonalds that sat just off the gas station property like a young sibling wanting to play with an older brother but not allowed, so he sat as close as possible hoping to eventually be included. The old road sported no sidewalk, so I ambled along the dusty shoulder, not worried about traffic since it appeared this road would get little, if any.

Another country lane. It wasn't noon yet, I had only been out of Chicago for 27 hours, and I was suddenly sick of quaint country lanes, with their weathered fences, tired farm houses, and brown carved land extending toward the horizon. It struck me as ironic that one could drive a day and find a scene that looked identical to one from the day before, that the defining hallmark of middle America was its consistency and conformity. When you all have the same town, the same land, the same houses, the same restaurants, the same shopping – well, not only are you always home, but you're never envious of anyone else. It's impossible to feel the need to "keep up with the Jones's" when the Jones's car and house and dog are a mirror image of yours. Of course, there's always the question of Jones' wife . . . while the exteriors and the environment echo each other, the people inhabiting that environment are different; different dreams, habits, likes, angers, passions. I wonder what dreams were lying behind the doors of the house right here? I wonder what dreams may have died behind those doors because there were no more colors in the box of crayons in this part of the world.

Did any people here decide to pull up stakes and move across country? And then I thought, did any people land here due to their decision to pull up stakes and move across country? Was this the "destination dream" of anyone? Does anyone dream of exchanging their "sameness" for a sameness in a different place? Is the Applebee's in Springfield any better or bolder or more hopeful than the Applebee's in, say, Joplin? Tulsa? Carbondale?

No surprises. People don't want surprises. People – most people – don't want to explore, try new things, have new experiences. Probably why vanilla is still the most popular ice cream flavor in the world. Stick with the devil you know.

Well, I can't do that anymore. Even though Chicago is certainly not Springfield, or Joplin, or anything remotely like this small dot on a map, it was still the devil I knew. I was ready for new – new sights, new smells, and maybe even a new devil. Funny, I asked for chocolate and was given rocky road.

And then I made my way here, and was violently reminded of the time and place when vanilla was the first flavor I ever tasted, when vanilla exciting and new. Not that Natalie was vanilla; no, it was the time of life, the things I – we – were growing into and experiencing for the first time, it was the flowering of our relationships with the people in our environment, that was when we started to view our existing, same world with new eyes, and began to taste the new flavors that had been in front of us, unknowingly, for our whole lives. At certain times of your life, you can see the familiar with new eyes and it all looks different. Whether it's from growing up, some event that changes you, or just acquiring a new perspective, one day you'll see things, the same old things, differently.

And when you do, you either appreciate them for what they now are, or you change your environment. You change your life.

Sunshine, just like Amy said. A new day, a new sun.

Walking down that street, it occurred to me that I had a habit of opening my eyes, looking at my reality with fresh vision, and then once it became uncomfortable I'd change that reality by changing my environment. It could be breaking up with someone you love, it could be by driving away someone you love, or it could be by simply leaving someplace you've always loved, someplace that, while home, now had too much of a backstory to be comfortable with. And it made me think about what Amy had said last night (and about what Elena had said the night before): was I just running away from something (or some things) instead of running toward something? Natalie . . . college out-of-state . . . living in the city instead of my childhood home town . . . Sarah . . . now this . . . I stopped and thought for a second: what's been driving my choices? Wanting something new, wanting to live life? Or wanting to be free of something old, and wanting to escape life? Was I coming or was I going?

I made my way back to my car, and, after grabbing a cup of coffee from McDonalds, jumped back on the expressway. It was nearing 11:00, late morning, and I was only 40 miles past Springfield, which meant, according to my calculations, there was no way I was making it to Amarillo tonight. Depending on road conditions, weather, construction, . . . it looked like Oklahoma City would be tonight's way station. Which was fine, I'd rather stop in a larger city than Springfield (there were smaller cities?), and as far as I know I didn't know anyone there. Of course, that's what I thought about Springfield, and look what that turned into.

The miles passed easily. The southwestern Missouri hills gently rolled past, and as I entered Joplin the sun snuck behind a bank of clouds, where it remained until I crossed the border into Oklahoma, which greeted me with myriad signs proclaiming not only native tribal lands (which I was now crossing) but also native tribal casinos (which I should stop at for MY CHANCE TO WIN BIG!). Just looking out my windows, if I had napped for the last hour and just woken I'd have no idea I was in a different state, as so far, Oklahoma was nothing more than Missouri with larger and bolder signage.

I was about to reach the outskirts of Tulsa (woo-hoo?) when my phone chirped. I looked down: Dan. I pressed to answer via the car phone speakers.

"Hey," I said "What's up?"

"So where are ya," he replied, eschewing any formalities.

"Nearing Tulsa."

"Isn't that on the east side of the state?"

"Yup."

"So what happened," he asked, "you get a late start this morning?"

"You'll never believe last night," I said, and I proceeded to tell him the whole story of Amy, Natalie, and my trip to a Camdenton cemetery. By the time I was done, and had answered most of his questions, I was almost through Tulsa. I pulled off the expressway at an exit with a sign extolling various fuel and food stops, and continued talking as I pulled into a Starbucks parking lot.

When I finished, he was silent for a moment before saying, "Jesus, what a night. So, how are you with all of this, you okay?"

"Yeah," I said, "I'm okay. I mean, while all the news and the rigmarole around it was a bit of a shock and distraction, it's not like I was physically harmed or unable to drive."

"Yeah, but I'd be so thrown by it all I'm not sure I could concentrate on the long drive," he said. "I almost think, if it was me, I'd stop now, or I wouldn't have gone on. I mean, you could've stayed at your cousin's place another night, right? So you lose a day, no big thing, not like Arizona won't be there when you get there."

"I thought about that," I replied, "but I didn't want to just sit and wallow in it all day. I did stop and take a walk after I left the cemetery, I mean, I kinda needed to, to clear my head, but other than that, no reason to just sit and think about it all day. Might as well drive, I mean, I can think about it when driving too, at least this way I get somewhere."

"That's logical," Dan said, "but what happened was too emotional for you to be thinking so logical. That's why you probably should stop, sit, and take time to come to grips with this."

"It would be different if it were Sarah, . . . or my sister, . . .or you, someone who's been close to me for the last five years. But as important as she was when I was in high school, it's not like this was a person who impacted my life immediately right now. It was, it was really out-of-the-blue, and it was sad as hell, but it's not something that's going to bring my life, or my day, to a grinding halt." I took a breath. "It made me, it makes me, terribly sad, especially in that I can never see her again or talk to her again, but . . . . "

Dan interjected. "And it makes you sad that, since you're now available, and you found out she was always available, and now that she's gone nothing can ever happen again. Just when you were free for a second chance, she's not there. And that's what's gonna sink in later."

And I had no reply to that. I sat silent, and chewed on my lip.

"You still there," Dan asked, "Or did you drive behind a butte?"

"No, still here, just pondering."

"Well, don't ponder too much, pay attention."

"I am," I said, "Just thinking that I'm not sure about the whole idea of me being affected by a latent desire to go back and be with Nat. I mean, I was moving away. Once Sarah and I were done, I still never thought of her, not that way, I always assumed she was happily married and all with her own life. A "Nat and Wade reunion" wasn't at the top of my to-do list."

"No, but now that you know, you probably can't help but fill in the blanks of what might have been."

I sighed. "True. But that still doesn't make it something that keeps me from driving forward."

"We can see that now, can't we," Dan said with humor in his voice. "Anything else up? Car surviving? All else good?"

"Livin' the dream, mile after mile of bliss and wonder."

"Who can ask for more, right?"

"You bet," I replied. "But hey, just stopped, need gas and food."

"Okay, right, you go," he said. "You need anything, let me know."

"Will do."

"Okay then, I'll talk to ya later."

"Later." And I clicked off.

It was just past 2:00 in the afternoon. I filled the car with gas, washed the windshield, and punctuated it all with a sip of my iced green tea. I had also taken the time to research and book a hotel for that night, a reasonably safe looking Embassy Suites on the north side of Oklahoma City. All that remained for me was to get to Oklahoma City and find it.

I had just turned the key in the ignition when my phone chirped, this time indicating a text message. I took a look and saw an unread message from Elena. One click and I read:

Hey you. How's the trip? Didn't decide to turn around and head back, did ya? Well, even if you didn't, I'm thinking about you. Hope you're safe and having fun. Write back! Miss ya already. E

I stifled my impulse to immediately respond, and decided it would be better for me to drive awhile, reach my day's destination, then maybe call and let her know how things have been. Well, maybe not let her know everything, but at least let her know I'm safe.

Again, the miles passed. The terrain evened, hills and valleys becoming less frequent, fewer groves of colored ashes or maples, more open land. It was easy to see why, almost a century ago, this part of the country became known as the "dust bowl," as there were times when I could see for miles and miles with no buildings, no trees, nothing visible that might have held the land in place. Farms passed, but by this point in the year they held little more than scraps of the harvest, the brown veins of turned land mingling with pale yellow debris. Here and there a lone tractor sat, old and rusted, an heirloom to a time when farming was not only profitable, but an essential way of life for Oklahomans. Now, over a decade into the 21st century, farming was a corporate endeavor, leaving little land (or hope) for independent farmers or tribal farms. For over an hour, the drive was bleak, and made me feel for those who had been raised on this land, and for those who were still trying to live and raise families here.

The air was getting crisp and the sun fading as I passed more buildings, more homes, more traffic. Soon the gentle colors of landscape were replaced by the brick and glass and steel of industrial and business centers, and the only growing things I saw were tall weeds sprouting from cracks in the median. Welcome to Oklahoma City.

If you've never been to Oklahoma City, then you're missing out on the country's largest city, size-wise. You're also missing out on the nightmarish fun of traffic that it includes, since most everyone within the county works somewhere in the city, yet nobody lives near where they work. The result is a highly complex series of roads, interchanges, and under/overpasses that can get you anywhere, as long as you know how to use them and know exactly where you're going. Oh, and if it's rush hour? You're not getting anywhere quickly.

I entered the city from the northeast. My hotel was on the northwest. Seemed like it would be easy, but achingly slow traffic, combined with roads that have different names live than they do on GPS, made for a comic series of turns, miscues, and backtracks. It was almost an hour for me to actually find the Embassy Suites; when I did, I almost jumped out of the car and blessed the parking lot. I grabbed my bag and made my way inside.

Once checked in, I found my room. Upon entering, I hit the button to liven my phone, figuring I should take the time now to get back to Elena. The iPhone sprang to life with the notices that I had 3 missed text messages and 1 missed call. I turned the phone to look at the volume button: off. Damn. So I clicked the messages icon to see what I missed. One from Amy, just checking to see how I'm doing. But 2 from my sister Beth. The first one, from about 2 hours ago, was simple: *Call me ASAP.* The second message was from about 40 minutes ago, and again fairly direct: *Really need to talk, call when you can.* I exited the message app and checked my missed call. Also Beth, no message. Which worried me; three tries to contact me, something must be up.

I hit redial from her call log, and the phone rang. Three rings later, Beth answered.

"Don't you read your messages or have your phone with you?" was how she greeted me.

"Sorry, I was driving and had the volume down from earlier so I didn't hear the messages or phone. What's up?"

"Mom," she said, as if I could discern every possible concern or issue from that single word.

"She calling you and leaning on you already since I left yesterday? You already tired of hearing from her?"

"No, her condo burned down."

Okay, that changed things. "Holy crap, is she okay?"

"Yeah. She's fine," Beth said, "but she's freaked out."

"Well yeah, no kidding. So what happened, what . . . I mean, burned down? Like, gone?" My mom lived in a mid-rise condo building, 6

55

stories, and she was on the fourth floor, near the elevator. It was a mix of older people, like her, and young couples or families with small kids, and it had a room on the first floor that housed all the laundry facilities for the entire complex. She loved it there for two reasons: it was a security building, and she had a group of ladies there that she was friends with that got together for coffee each day at 4:00 to sit and talk and update each other on their various maladies. She'd been there for 7 years, and she didn't want to go anywhere else.

Beth said, "So I guess, from what mom said, someone in one of the third floor units decided to use a space heater, you know, one of those portable things? And the person turned it on too close to their draperies, and then fell asleep, and it caught the drapes on fire."

"Jesus."

"Yeah, smart people there. So anyway, suddenly the wall was on fire, and then the floor was full of smoke, and one of the neighbors was coming home and saw and smelled the smoke, and then called the fire department. By the time the firemen got there, the fire had spread, and people were panicking, and mom must've had her hearing aid out, because she didn't hear a thing at first . . . "

"When did this happen, what time of day?"

"Early morning, about 7:00. Anyway, mom said she thought she smelled something, like someone was doing a lot of cooking, and then after a bit people banged on her door to get her out of there."

"What about the smoke alarms, didn't she hear them?"

"She says she didn't," Beth replied. "You know her, she's as good as deaf without the hearing aids. So her neighbors helped her out of the building, down the stairs, and they all watched while the firemen took care of the fire."

"How bad's the building," I asked, "I mean, can she still live there? Did the whole thing burn down, or just that unit, ya know, is she able to go back, how bad is it?"

Heavy sigh from Beth. "Well," she sighed again, "Mom's going to be staying with us for a while. They let people in later in the day to get clothes, phones, medicine, essentials, but the building's not safe right now for occupancy. It's still there, and it's not a total loss, but there's enough damage, especially to the third floor, that it'll be a while, maybe a month or more, til she can live there again."

"Oh, geez," I said. "So . . . yikes. Well, at least you're there and you have room."

"Yeah, and it won't be too bad for a short while. And in a way she'll be happy, since she'll get to see Julia all the time now." Julia was Beth's 4-year-old daughter, my mom's only grandchild, and the light of my mom's life.

"Well, at least she's okay, that's the main thing."

"Yeah, but she's also worried and anxious, she really wasn't able to get everything she wanted out of her place. They only gave her about 5 minutes to get essentials, and now that she's here and has had some time to think and ponder, she wishes she'd taken some of dad's things, mementos, jewelry, that sort of stuff. Oh, and pictures, she's now panicky about all her pictures still being there."

"Well yeah, that's all she has left of dad, her parents, that sort of thing, I can imagine she'll be a basket case til she can get in and make sure some of that's okay."

Beth took a deep breath. "She'll live, it'll all be there when she gets back."

"And big picture, she's okay, and it wasn't her unit that went up in flames."

"Right. So where are you now?"

"Oklahoma City."

"I thought you'd be farther, given how fast you drive."

Funny lady, that Beth. I told her about my evening in Springfield, and about the news about Natalie. "So I'm a bit behind schedule, and a bit pre-occupied the past 24 hours."

"Wow, no kidding. She was really young, that's so sad. And you haven't seen her in years, have you."

"Nope."

"Well, I feel for you, and I feel for her family and her cousin, too, that's gotta be rough to deal with."

"Not something you ever plan for or prepare for." I hadn't told Beth about my conversation (or monologue, if you will) at Beth's grave site. I figured that's a piece of history between Natalie and myself, and it was best to keep it that way. No need to delve into it all at this late date. "But, at least today, and for me, life does go on."

"Yup," she replied. "Gotta keep going."

"Which I did, albeit a bit behind schedule. But no worries, I'll make it there just fine. Meanwhile, anything else comes up with mom, or you need anything, let me know."

"You gonna turn your volume up now?"

"Ha ha, yes, I'll do that," I said. "Is mom there now?"

"She's in her new room, but she's resting right now."

"Probably best," I said. "Let her know I called."

"I will do that," Beth said, "and I'll let her know she can call you if she wants."

"That's fine, not sure I'll be doing much except having dinner and then watching hotel room TV tonight."

"Okay, well," she said, "have a good night, and drive safe tomorrow."

"Will do. Give mom a hug for me and tell her I'm glad she's safe."

"I will. Talk to you later."

"Bye." And I clicked off. Geez, as if not enough has happened the last few days, now my mom's condo complex catches fire? I almost said out loud "What's next," but I thought the better of challenging the gods to come up with something else larger in scale.

I quickly unpacked a few items I'd need for the night and morning and then decided I'd find someplace to eat. I hadn't noticed many restaurants in the area save for the usual middle-class suburban chains that grew like weeds (yup, another Applebee's right across the parking lot). I figured I had the time to drive around a bit, explore, and see what I could find that looked promising.

What I discovered is that as confusing a jumble the Oklahoma City expressways were, they were nothing compared to the side streets and neighborhood throughways. I got stuck on one-way roads twice, both times taking me away from where I wanted to head. I discovered numerous streets that simply ended, leaving my choice of right or left being dictated by whichever lane I happened to be in. I was cut off by trucks, sedans, and motorcycles, all of them blessed with the knowledge of how to get from point A to point B in this town, something I'd gladly pay to know. And I passed the same mall three times, each time from a different direction. At the last pass, I decided to continue straight on the road I was on, and see where it led and what I'd find.

What I found, after 15 minutes of stop-and-go driving, was a small, non-descript joint with a subtle sign that read "El Viajero," had plenty of well cared-for cars out front, and was infusing the air with incredible aromas of barbacoa and carnitas. I pulled in, locked the car, and entered through the ornately carved wooden door.

A smiling senorita greeted me at the door and led me to a small table, out of the way and near the windows. I scanned the menu, decided on a plate of the steak street tacos and a Negro Modelo, and started mindlessly munching on the chips and hot salsa that was placed in front of me. The place was warm and homey, reminding me of one of the many small, authentic Mexican places that my friends and I haunted on Chicago's north side, the type of place where the head chef was often a mother or grandmother cooking recipes handed down from her mother or grandmother, often done completely by memory, no written record of it in existence.

I thought of those restaurants, and of how I came to be so adoring of Mexican and Tex-Mex food - - and barbeque, and Indian food, and Mediterranean, . . . many styles and cultures of food that were not familiar in my suburban neck of the world when growing up. In fact, my mother and father were very basic and utilitarian when it came to food for the family, whether cooking at home or dining out. "What's wrong with good old American food," my father would roar when my sister and I made pleas for dinner at Chi Chi's, or wanted Taco Bell instead of McDonalds. My mother considered spaghetti or pizza to be ethnic foods, and anything more exotic would be met with shakes of her head, her wondering what got into us and why we needed something so crazy.

Crazy. To my mother, linguine with marinara sauce was crazy.

I remembered a time, shortly after Sarah and I were engaged, when we took my mother out to dinner. My father had just gone into assisted care for his Parkinson's, and we thought taking my mom out for a nice dinner would be a good break for her, from all the stress she'd been dealing with. We chose a cute little Chinese place in downtown Geneva, *Canton Chef*, a place that had been there as long as I could remember and had become a favorite of Sarah and me. My mom was game, but once seated and staring at the menu it was obvious that she had no idea what was what, or what to do.

"How do you know what to order," she asked. "All these items, I have no idea what they are except for when it says chicken or beef or shrimp."

I walked her through the menu, what the various titles like Kung Pao or General Tsing meant, what the little pepper meant, and how most of the dishes were only different based on whether you wanted rice or noodles. "How did you learn all of this," she said, "this is like a different language. Did they teach this in school, we never learned anything like this."

Sarah stifled a bit of a chuckle, and I just smiled. "Mom, the way you learn is going out and trying new things. I went out with friends, other people, . . . you go out and try things and learn, it's no big thing."

"Well I'm not sure I could do it," she declared. "Your father and I, we had the places we liked, and he had his favorite foods, he was a steak and potatoes man, so we ate in normal, regular American places, we didn't go for all these exotic foods from China or Japan or Spain. We liked the foods we grew up eating, and that was good old meat and potatoes." She took a sip of water. "Why not just stay with the things you like? Why isn't that good enough anymore?"

Sigh. It sometimes made me rather sad, her not wanting to "spread her wings" and try new things, but then I decided that if she was happy in her comfort zone, why push things. Didn't mean I couldn't try new things.

My Negro Modelo arrived, and the dark-haired waitress smiled and poured it into a glass for me. I sipped; yup, after this day that was just what I needed. My thoughts returned to my mom, and gravitated from her lack of cultural culinary knowledge to her simple yet genuine outlook on life, and a conversation we shared when I first moved out from Sarah. She had sensed something wasn't right between the two of us, particularly that something wasn't right with me, but she hadn't said anything until I brought it up one night at her place. After I told her that Sarah and I were having problems, and that I was moving out for a bit because I needed time and space and I thought Sarah deserved as much, she nodded as if the news wasn't unexpected.

"I'm not surprised," she said. "There was always something, really as soon as you two were married, you didn't seem right."

"What do you mean, didn't seem right? Like depressed, or angry or something? Because if that's the case you were reading something that wasn't there."

"No, it wasn't like that," she said, "it was that you'd say you'd call, but then you wouldn't for a few weeks. Or we'd go a month or two sometimes without seeing you. You'd be having her family over, or going to family gatherings with her family, but not doing that with your family. It just seemed like once you and Sarah got married, you spent more time with her family, that's all. And I figured you were doing that because that's what she wanted, but after a couple of years when that was still happening, I figured either you wanted it that way, or you just didn't know how to change it."

"But why didn't . . ."

"Why didn't I ever say anything?" She finished my sentence for me. "Because it wasn't my place. You're an adult, it was your life, and I wasn't about to be the interfering mother or mother-in-law and start complaining about how little we saw of you. I figured it would work itself out, one way or the other. And," she paused, "it apparently has, maybe not with the answer you were looking for, but with the answer you needed to find. It's tough, but you're where you are for a reason."

"Well, this sucks," I replied. "I wish someone would've said something earlier."

"Would it have made a difference?" After a few seconds of silence, she continued. "You were going to do what you were going to do, and if anyone said anything, you would have told them to go jump in a lake, and you know it. And who knows, maybe it might've worked itself out, and I would've been wrong, which would've been fine with me, I'd rather have been wrong and saved you the pain. But it is what it is."

"Well hell."

She smiled. "You'll get through this, kiddo, you always get through things when things are tough. Just have faith, don't beat yourself up over it, and move on."

I was playing that part of the conversation through in my mind – "don't beat yourself up over it" – when the waitress brought out my steaming plate of food. Again with a smile as grand as Jalisco itself, she set the plate down, asked if there was anything else I needed, and when assured there wasn't went about her way in a twirl of multicolored skirt ruffles.

The food was good, the right amount of spice and heat balanced by the right amount of cool from the salsa. It was better than I might have expected from anywhere in Oklahoma, and perhaps because of that it was that much more enjoyable. The waitress returned after maybe three bites to inquire if everything was to my liking. My response – "oh yes, very much" – pleased her, and she left with the same wide smile that she'd sported the entire night, making me wonder if it was real or something tattooed on prior to her shift.

Despite the solace the tacos provided, my thoughts kept returning to my mother, the fire earlier today, and our relationship over the recent years. It was so cliché and common how I thought so little of her by the time I hit my teens and beyond, and it was a refreshing awakening to learn, as I matured, that she wasn't the complete bumpkin that I had always assumed. Oh, she had her moments, and she was never the most cultured or worldly of people, but within her innocence she held a sharp insight into people, particularly those close to her. Both Beth and I had been surprised and dumbfounded by her sporadic bouts of deep insight and understanding of us, our lives, and our interpersonal situations. More than once I was rendered speechless by something she said that I would've expected from a trained psychological therapist.

Three nights before I left, I had dinner with her along with Beth, her daughter Julia, and Beth's husband Aaron. We ate at her favorite restaurant, a diner-type establishment optimistically named "Winners Circle" that had been hanging on for a dozen years. It was meant to be a going away dinner, a celebration of me taking a step into the unknown and branching out to something new. But for some reason, which I still cannot put my finger on, my mother decided that it was more of a sad occasion than a happy one. Sure, I was leaving town, which was sad for her. But she attacked it as though it was an affront to her, the family (what was left of it), and common sense in general.

"I really don't know why you feel the need to leave," she said between spoonfuls of soup. "Just because you and Sarah are split up doesn't mean one of you needs to leave town."

"Well, sure, I know that" I said, "it's not a matter of needing to leave to get away from Sarah, it's a need that I feel right now to go somewhere else and, well, not really start over, but re-start, or just shake up the norm and be somewhere else, somewhere new, somewhere without the history. I really think this is a good time, a definite transition in my life, where if I'm going to do this, this is the perfect time."

"But why so far away," she asked, "why not somewhere closer where we could still see you every now and then, maybe Milwaukee, or somewhere in Indiana? Indiana's nice."

"Come on, mom," Beth said, "Indiana's not the sort of place you go running to to start over."

"What's wrong with Indiana?" Mom asked.

I jumped in. "Nothing's wrong with Indiana, nothing's wrong with Milwaukee, it's just not what I want right now. I'd rather go somewhere that feels different, looks different, has a different pace and rhythm of life."

"It's his life," Beth added, "he should be able to move where he wants."

"But it's so far," mom said. "Arizona, that's . . . that's time zones away. I remember your grandmother saying she always had a difficult time calling people in Arizona because she never knew what time it was there. Plus it's so hot there in the desert."

"Sedona's not in the desert," I said, "it's about an hour-and-a-half north of Phoenix, higher in the mountains, so it's warm but not hot, and they even get snow in the winter, so it's not some desert oven."

Aaron piped in, "Yeah, I've heard it's beautiful there, red rocks, I think that's what they have, supposed to be gorgeous scenery. Take pictures and send 'em back to us."

Mom was quiet for a moment, then let out an audible sigh. "So you'll go out there and never come back, and I'll never see you again. Will you at least come back for my funeral?"

"Oh, for crying out loud, . . ."

"Geez mom," Beth said, "he's not going to the moon, he's just going to another state. They have airports and train stations and highways, so he can get back here whenever he wants and it won't be a problem."

"And seriously, I'm not going away forever," I said. "Kids, people move away all the time. Like when I went away for college, I was away, that was the point."

"And you came back," she replied with a tone of righteous authority. "That's what kids do, they go away to college, come home in the summer, and then when they graduate they go wherever the jobs are, and in your case jobs were available back home, so you came home where you belonged."

"Well ma, I'm not sure I belong here anymore," I said. "At least, not now. Who knows, maybe again someday, but not now." I tried to punctuate that proclamation with a bite of my BLT, but mom was unimpressed.

"Are you scared of running into Sarah or her parents?" she asked.

"No," I replied, "Doesn't bother me . . ." (okay, slight lie) ". . . and even here in town it's a big world, chances of us happening across one another are pretty slim, I would think."

"You shouldn't run away just to avoid people," she said.

"Mom, I'm not trying to avoid Sarah, or her parents. Jeez, it's over, we're all moving forward. She, her family, they can stay here or go wherever they want, do whatever they want, to move forward, that's, . . . that's fine, that's their call. Me, I want to go somewhere else. I want to surround myself with new sights, new sounds, a new environment." I paused and looked at her. "The best way for me to re-build myself is to do it somewhere else, somewhere new."

My mom gently placed her spoon on the saucer. "Well, when I'm sick and your sister is forced to take care of me all by herself, I'm sure you'll wish you were back here."

Guilt trip. As if on cue.

"Mom, don't you want me to be happy?"

"Oh Wade," she said, "Of course I want you to be happy, and I really think splitting from Sarah, while it's difficult, is the first step to you being happy. But I think happiness comes from inside, not from where you live. I think you can be just as happy here as you can anywhere else."

"But don't I deserve the chance to find that out myself?"

"Well," she said, pausing and looking for a word or a thought, "can't you just, I don't know, visit there for a week or two and see what you think before moving all the way across the country? This sudden decision to move out there seems so final, especially since you don't know anyone there. I'll worry about you being all alone far from home."

"Mom, he's a big boy," Beth added. "He'll be fine, and we'll be fine, and he'll visit, and everything will work out just great."

"Oh I know he will, but I'll miss him. It's so nice having you here, that I'll miss you not being around, I'll miss not being able to see you often."

The whole conversation was in that vein, Mom wishing out loud that I wouldn't go. And in that process, she laid a lot of guilt on me. And that's something else I was feeling right now, with me sitting here in a Mexican café in Oklahoma City, and her staying with Beth due to a fire in her building. I could have been there for her. Maybe I should have been there for her. I know when I talk to her, she'll again tell me she wishes I was there. But the truth is that there's nothing right now I could do any differently whether I was here or there. If I was in Chicago, she'd still be staying with Beth, and I'd still be out having dinner, only probably not alone.

So why the guilt? Why this feeling that I've let her down by not being there for her? She didn't do this when I went to college, nor did she do this when I married Sarah and we moved to the city, a 30-mile distance that felt culturally and socially farther than the mapped miles. And while

I have no knowledge of this, I don't believe she did this when Beth went to college (admittedly, Northern Illinois University is only an hour from the family abode in Geneva) nor when Beth married Aaron and they moved a 30 minute drive north.

I would venture a guess that this move of mine, at this time of her life, is much different than past family relocations partly due to my father now being gone. When Parkinson's finally took him, it left Beth and I (and our spouses, and eventually her granddaughter) as the primary focus of her life, the ones that not only meant the most to her, but upon whom her life revolved around. While she was still relatively healthy for her age, still driving, still mobile, she was slowing down. She had a hearing aid now, which she constantly forgot to load with batteries, making it fairly useless. Her hair had turned gray, her walk had slowed, and she stood a bit more stooped than earlier years. But her mind had remained sharp (or at least sharp relative to her previous self), and she could still read people better than most people I know. She was aging, and that wasn't pleasant, especially when your chosen partner didn't live up to his end of the bargain to gracefully age with you, but she was doing well. So why the sudden need for me to be in the area? Beth was still there, her granddaughter was still there. Why was I necessary too?

Yes, of course, I'm her son, her first-born, and that's always going to carry an emotional weight that defies logic. And I suppose now with dad gone, I'm the ranking male in the family, the alpha dog, and it's tough for the pack to function with the alpha dog gone. Yet creating one's own life, even if it means doing so elsewhere, is part of life. Mom conveniently forgets that she raised her family in a different state than where she was raised, and her mom was raised halfway across the country before marrying her dad. Moving away, for love or job or simple wanderlust, is something of the norm these days, not something destructive to families or threatening to a way of life. People moved around, but they didn't lose where they were from, nor the part of their environmental upbringing that helped shape them and make them who they are.

Aargh. Whatchagonnado?

I looked down at my now empty plate. Where the hell did all the tacos go? Damn. I hope I enjoyed them. That's what I get for pondering conversations with mom while eating.

The raven haired waitress came back. "All done, you liked it?"

"Yes, very much, it was very good."

She smiled so big I thought her face would break. "Wonderful, I'm so glad." She scooped up the plate and silverware and hustled it away to a waiting sink. When she returned with the check, I quickly gave her my debit card, and she again swept away cheerfully to take care of it. I was one part impressed, one part amused at her full throttle energy she put into her duties, and I hoped that it resulted in her raking in ample tip money every night. When she returned, she placed the tray and bill in front of me and again offered that it was great to have me here, and she sincerely hoped I had a good dinner and experience.

"It was more than wonderful," I told her, "and you were wonderful."

She smiled, and said "Oh, thank you."

"So," I continued, "I'd like to stop for maybe one more drink before heading home, but I'm not from around here," and as I was speaking she started blushing, as if I were just another guy passing through town hitting on her. "No, no, I just wanted, was hoping you could suggest a quiet place between here and the interstate where I could stop for a drink, that's all."

She tilted her head, and said, "Uhm, for you, I think Tornado Alley Brewery and Grill would be perfect."

"For me, okay, I'll take that as I hope it's meant." I listened as she told me how to get there, and I thanked her again. I signed the bill, included a generous tip, and then made my way out. As I passed her near the door I again said, "Thank you, have a great evening." She replied in kind. I pushed the door open and exited into the cool Oklahoma night.

I smiled as I got into my car and fired it up. It was, despite my contemplation of all things mother, a good night, much better (so far) than last night. I was fairly certain that my waitress was not related to any past girlfriends, ex-wife, family, . . . and I was certain that I would have a night that would allow me to mentally escape the turmoil, the cacophony, of the past 48 hours. All I needed – all I wanted – was one final nightcap, and then a warm bed all to myself.

I had no sooner started the car than my phone rang, the familiar ring tone I assigned to my Mom. I clicked it to answer.

"Hey, Mom, how are you doing? I talked to Beth earlier, are you alright?"

"Oh, it's been quite a day," she replied, her voice weary with fatigue. "I'm just glad to be alive at this point." Already playing up the 'woe is me.'

"Oh my, I thought Beth said that the fire was on the third floor and that the whole building didn't burn, just that part of it."

"Well, the fire was on the third floor," she began to speak, making it obvious to me that her hearing aid wasn't in, "and you know, that's right below me. And I was asleep, because it was morning, and I guess the woman in the unit below me placed a portable heater too close to her curtains and it caught fire."

"Right, right," I said, "but your floor didn't catch fire did it?"

"No, my floor wasn't the one on fire, it was the third floor, but we still got a lot of smoke up here, and some people on my floor were saying they could feel the fire through the floor, and one person who's unit is directly above the fire did get some damage, so we could've been really harmed by this."

"But you're safe, and that's important."

"Well yes, but now I have no place to live until they get the building inspected or fixed or whatever they need to do to it, so I have to stay with Beth and Aaron for a while."

"At least you have someone there," I said, "you do have someplace you can stay for as long as you need to."

"We had to wait to get back in, and I needed to get all my medicine, and then some clothes, so Edna, the condo board president who lives on the second floor, was even wondering if they'd let us in for that, it was so bad."

"But they did let you in, right?"

"Oh yes, they had to, I think, or people would've been angry. They can't keep us from medicine, I know Evelyn, my neighbor down the hall, she has pills she had to take and was afraid she'd be missing her time to take them, so she was worried."

"So mom, do you have everything you need? All your medicine, clothes, anything else? Phone book, everything?"

Another weary sigh. "Oh yes, I think I'm okay. I hope they let us go back soon, I don't want to be a bother, and it's inconvenient for everybody, I don't want to be in the way."

"Look at the bright side, you get to have a lot of time with Julia for a while, that's good, right?"

"Oh she's been such a sweetie," mom gushed, "she wanted to be a doctor and examine me to make sure Grandma was okay, then she brought me cookies and milk to make me feel better, and then she gave me one of her stuffed animals and told me to take a nap, so Julia's taking care of her grandma."

"Well, that's great, I'm sure everybody there is taking good care of you."

"And are you okay," she asked, "you're not turning around because of the fire, are you, I'll be okay here with Beth and Aaron so there's no real need for you to come back or anything, I'll be fine."

"No mom, I'm fine, I'm far on my way, I'm in Oklahoma City tonight, and by tomorrow night I'll be in New Mexico, so . . ."

"Oooh, Oklahoma City," she broke in, "You're really getting there aren't you, you've gone pretty far so far. Well, I can see why it wouldn't make sense for you to come back, there's really nothing you can do here, and I'll be fine with Beth and Aaron."

"Right, right," I said, "but I will call you tomorrow to see how you are, and I'll talk to you every day until you get back into your place, I don't want to have to worry about you."

"Oh, you don't worry about me, you just keep going and I'll be just fine."

And it was right about then that it really started annoying me that she called to see if she could talk me into coming back to Chicago. Her subtle 'you're not turning around, are you' was just her way of really saying she was hoping I had already turned around and was hurrying home to . . . what, exactly? What could I do there that Beth wasn't already doing? Yet here she was, dropping all these hints that she wished I'd come back, and then the very passive-aggressive phrase turn of 'there's no need for you to come back, I'll be fine.' Yes, I was worried about her, but much less worried knowing that she was safe, and was with Aaron and Beth. And now that worry was dissipating and being replaced with annoyance that she wasn't so much wanting to know how I am, or how the trip is going, as it was her wanting me to know she wanted me back there.

"So anything else right now mom? I'm heading back to my hotel after dinner, and I don't want to get lost or distracted." Okay, white lie, but totally warranted.

"Oh no, you drive, and be careful. I just wanted you to know that I was okay, and for you not to worry or change your plans."

"Okay, well I'm glad you're okay," I said. "I'll let you get some rest, and I'll call you tomorrow when I stop for the night."

"Okay honey, you do that. Love you."

"Love ya too, Mom." I clicked to hang up. Okay, now I definitely needed a nightcap. Off to Tornado Alley Brewery and Grill.

It was easy to find and easy to spot, and with the amount of neon showering the building I'm rather sure it could be seen from space on a clear night. Being a Saturday night the lot was crowded, and as I made my way inside I had to wander the floor for a few minutes until I found an empty spot at the bar. I settled in, and when the bartender stopped by I ordered bourbon on the rocks. He went off to get it, and I sat back to take in the bar, the people, and the TV sets that were again blasting college football in every corner of the building. He quickly returned with my drink and asked if I wanted to start a tab. I told him that would be a great idea, and he took my credit card to run and hold. So far, so good.

Tornado Alley Brewery and Grill had the same vibe that I had seem time and time again throughout the suburban brewpubs that ringed Chicago. There were dozens of large-screen TVs, all turned to sports; there were chalkboards on the walls with colorful handwritten descriptions of the various beers on tap; there were tables of millennials in animated conversations, many of them sporting Oklahoma Sooners t-shirts or jerseys; and there was the ever-present smell of open fire cooked meat (burgers, steaks, ribs) that gently massaged the air. I was in Oklahoma City, but it could have been Florida, Colorado, Minnesota, or California. Carefully crafted and manufactured atmosphere.

As I sat and nursed my drink, the twenty-something couple seated to my right was having an increasingly animated conversation, apparently something to do with his refusal to cancel a weekend hunting trip with his friends that was clashing with a wedding expo she was expecting them to attend as a couple. As they spoke it became clear that neither of them was really interested in what the other thought, they simply wanted to have their way, and were both intent on "winning."

"You know it's the first weekend of hunting season," he was saying, "and you know that me and my brothers always go out the first weekend. It's family tradition."

"And what, if you don't go the first weekend one year all the deer are going to be gone, one year you can't put it off for a week for our wedding?"

"It's not our wedding," he countered, "it's some show you're all hyper about, and since it's probably all dresses and flowers and stuff that matters to you, you should still go, just go without me, take your sister or your mom or something, you'll still have a good time."

"Okay, you don't get it, it's something that the bride and groom are supposed to do together, *together*! You and I, not me and my sister."

He snorted and took a drag from his bottle of Bud Light. "C'mon, these things are scams anyway, they just wanna get you there to sell you a bunch of stuff you really don't need but once you see it, 'oh my God I can't live without it.' And they're geared toward women, so . . ."

"Hey, they have things there for guys too, I told you, DJs and music, limos, tuxes, it's not just for women. And this is *our* wedding, not just mine, I'd appreciate some input from you for some of this, like flowers, . . ."

"Ugh."

" . . . and like, don't ugh me, like the cake, the photographer, . . ."

"But see, that's the thing," he shot back, "we have a bakery two blocks from our place, my dad knows a photographer, we have all the stuff we need, a tux place, all that, we already have it near where we live, so why do we need to go and see all these people try to sell us on stuff? It makes no sense."

"It would be really nice if you took an interest in your own wedding," she said, "but no, instead it's more important for you to go out hunting that weekend. Well, fine." She crossed her arms and turned away from him. "Go, whatever, I don't care."

"Good."

"I'll go to the show without you and make all the choices myself, will you like that?"

"Hey, I trust whatever you choose," he replied. "Go for it."

She took a sip from her glass of white wine. "Fine, if this doesn't matter to you at all I'll just do it all myself."

"I don't know why you're getting so worked up about it, it's just a stupid show," he said, which was apparently the very wrong thing to say as she punctuated his words by hopping off her stool and stomping away. He watched her for a couple of seconds, and when she didn't turn around to come back he followed her, yelling, "God damn it Olivia, wait, come back."

Young love. Nothing like it.

I sipped more from my drink, and wondered what their lives would look like in a year, five years – hell, after listening to that, and how neither of them really wanted to listen to the other or compromise, I wondered what their lives would look like in 2 months. They seemed like so many of the young couples Sarah and I used to see on "House Hunters," her determined to get her thing, he determined to get his thing, the whole episode ending up looking like a precursor to an early divorce. Actually, thinking back, they sounded like a few arguments Sarah and I actually had, those where our sides and each of us "getting our way" took precedence over working things out together and meeting somewhere we could both be happy. The part of maturing – both as an individual, and as a couple – that was toughest to accept was that you don't always get what you want, you don't always get your way, and that doesn't mean you've lost anything, it actually means you're smart enough to understand that winning comes in all shapes and sizes. More often than not, losing out on "your way" mean winning in a larger sense.

I thought about times in the past I was sold on "winning" and how many times I ended up losing more than I had bargained for. The funny thing was, I eventually stopped "trying to win," and that led to me becoming too docile for my own good. I started swallowing my own wants and needs, and instead of trying to win or even compromise, my goal was to not have the other person (wife, mother, friend, co-worker) get upset with me for getting in their way of their winning. I'd give in before the issue came to a head; I'd keep my feelings bottled up; I'd let resentment simmer; I'd overflow with anger. And I destroyed things. Relationships.

Relationships – damn, I forgot to get back to Elena. Not that she and I were, . . . no, but we still had a relationship of some sort or the other, ill-defined, whatever one might want to call it. She texted earlier that day, I owed her a response. I pulled out my phone, found her message, and replied:

Hey, sorry, lot of driving today. Here safe in Ok City, been eventful, will need to tell you all about it. More driving tomorrow, hope to make it to NMex. Thanks for the thoughts, have a great night.

I clicked send. Then I flagged down the bartender and ordered another drink. And for a fleeting moment I wondered if what I was doing really was the right thing, if perhaps the stars and signs and karma itself was telling me that right now I didn't need to win and get my way, that right now I needed to compromise and be part of my family, part of my mom's life as she tried to rebuild what hadn't burned down.

No. It was time for me to do something for me. I'd deal with the guilt of leaving just as my mom needed her whole family. What was it that Dr. Wright had said? That there's no ideal time to do anything, so you just have to take a breath and do it? Well, this is my breath. This is my time.

Life was still messy, for me and those close to me (and near to me). Clarity, and Arizona, couldn't come soon enough.

Sunday, October 19

The house was dark, every hallway long and unending, and the footsteps echoed loudly even though I was standing still. I took a small step, then another; I reached out to the walls to guide me and steady me, but every time I reached out the wall seemed to move farther away, and every step closer to the wall was an illusion, the wall kept moving farther away. I inched closer, what I thought should be closer, but couldn't reach anything. I was reaching to the point of losing my balance, and before I could touch the wall a strong breeze came whistling down the hallway, curtains fluttering. The breeze strengthened, until it blew a picture free from its place on the wall, and when it fell the glass shattered, breaking the silence and triggering the breeze to halt.

I walked over to the remnants of the picture, but instead of glass there were pieces of paper on the ground. When I bend down to clean them up, I found they were scraps of my high school yearbook, scraps of pictures of Sarah and myself, scraps of a screenplay I wrote in college that never sold. I looked at each piece, trying to figure out why they were there, how they got there. I could recognize some of the words, and some of the people in the photos, but the colors were running, and soon the ink was all over my hands.

I stood and was no longer in the hallway, but instead was standing outside a modest white house, single story, covered in clapboard, surrounded by a petite lawn lush and green. A dog ran from behind the house to the left, and continued past me, disappearing to the right, as if he were running circles around the property and the yard. I walked to the mailbox, hoping I could hide some of the scraps there. The name on the mailbox — F. P. Errati — was printed in block letters. When I pulled the box door open, a bird flew out, I'm not sure what type of bird. It flew in tight circles around the yard, then swooped into the open window of the car in the driveway. I took a few steps toward the car; the window closed, and all I could see is my reflection, my face covered in a long, bushy beard, the type I've never been able to grow. When I reached up to touch it, I heard her voice: "Why did you let the bird out, you were supposed to keep it and protect it, but now it's gone." I turned toward the voice thinking "Natalie," and the yard spun. And all I saw then was his name again on the mailbox: F. P. Errati.

I woke with a jolt, not sure where I was or what time it was. The room was dark, my neck covered with sweat but my feet freezing cold. I looked over to my right, where in the past I've always found the glowing numbers of my clock, and saw the pale green readout that read *5:23*. I let my head fall back into the pillow. F. P. Errati: what the hell was that? Who the hell was that? And why was I in charge of caring for a bird in a mailbox? Too many questions for this early in the morning.

I tried to fall back asleep, but couldn't get comfortable, nor could I get some of the details of the dream out of my mind. None of the places were recognizable to me, at least not at that time. The voice, the voice . . . why did I think it was Natalie? No, couldn't be, but then who was it? Was it my Mom, my sister? Sarah? Elena? Someone else? Damn it, where have I heard that voice before, . . . think, think.

Damn it, who is F. P. Errati, and why was I at his house, his cute, perfect suburban house?

After thrashing about for what seemed like an eternity I again checked the time: *6:04*. Well, I wasn't going to be getting any more sleep, so I might as well get up, get myself going, and head west. I flipped on the light and saw the covers of the bed scrambled, as if a storm had passed through and left disheveled linens as wreckage. My pillow was moist, residue of the sweat covering my neck. I slowly stood and made my way to the shower, where I had high hopes that a hot shower would inject some life, as well as some answers, to my morning.

The hot water helped, as did the cup of coffee from the in-room maker. I dressed, double-checked for anything I might have forgotten, and then headed out. The morning was cool and the sun was rising over the eastern sky, bathing the parking lot, street, and buildings in a warm, optimistic blush. I felt surprisingly good, physically and mentally, and was hoping the day's drive would be uneventful.

I eased my car into the barely existent Sunday morning traffic, and carefully weaved my way from the feeder street onto the loop 44, which I would follow until it intersected with Route 40, which would be my route from here to Arizona. I drove cautiously, and was struck by the number of pickup trucks in the far left lane flying past the cars and semis in the right two lanes, as if having a gun rack in the back window and a confederate flag decal on the bumper gave one permission to drive 20-30 miles over the limit. It was a reminder that while Oklahoma as a state was too new to have been in the Confederacy, their leanings and kinships aligned with southerners, and they thought of themselves as southern, just like any good-ole-boy from Alabama or Mississippi. This despite the abundance of native tribal communities that flourished throughout the state. Cats and dogs living together in perfect (or not-so-perfect) harmony.

I found Route 40, eased onto it, and within 30 minutes was outside the city limits, nothing but low slung fields and farms passing along both sides of the concrete ribbon that stretched to the horizon. The more minutes passed, the fewer cars and trucks I saw, until the road held only a handful of vehicles, most of those being semis and tanker trucks. And as further miles passed, the fields became dotted with oil derricks, a reminder that this was the heart of oil country, and despite the rural nature of the environment there were probably more multi-millionaires in this area than in my old Chicago neighborhood.

After an hour I made a stop at a Citgo, refueled the car, and grabbed another cup of coffee. The morning that had begun with such energy was turning into a tiring slog, with nothing of interest outside my windows. I had traveled many times through Illinois, heading south to see friends at University of Illinois in Champaign/Urbana, and the joke was always that that drive was the most boring stretch of expressway in the country. Well, I think Route 40, west of Oklahoma City and not yet in Texas, could vie for that honor. Even on a sunny day it was tiring in its never-ending sameness and repetition. Brown fields, an oil rig, an old tractor, a farm house, ... repeat every ten miles.

Just over two-and-a-half hours after I left Oklahoma City, I saw the signs proclaiming that I was entering Texas. Well, funny thing, where that sign was placed everything looked exactly like Oklahoma. So it wasn't as if magic happened and things livened up. New state, but not much appeared different. The next sign let me know that Amarillo was a scant 100 miles away, which was great because that put me in a big town with real food and real amenities by lunch time.

Of course, Amarillo's a big town that desperately wants to be a city but is really still just a big town, sitting alone in the hilly panhandle of the state. Interstate 40 cuts directly through the center of Amarillo, affording travelers the opportunity to stop in at any one of a number of Texas-sized shops or restaurants, most famously The Big Texan. Nestled along the I-40 frontage road, surrounded by industrial buildings and only a block from a cemetery (which I'm sure comes in handy for those who try to down a 72 oz. steak in one sitting and inevitably fail), it was everything brassy and bold and boastful that defined Texas, from the giant rocking chair out front to the multiple state flags that ringed the building. Even at lunch time the lot was filled with SUVs, mini-vans, pickup trucks, and Cadillacs. Should you not want to partake of a gut-busting steak, but still feel the need to have a Big Texan t-shirt, hat, or shot glass, the Big Texan Gift Shop, right next door, would welcome you and your Visa card with Texas hospitality.

As I passed The Big Texan, all I could think was that it seemed calculated, phony, mercenary. I felt like I, along with every other traveler or vacationer that made it to Amarillo, was the currency of the town, and it felt uncomfortably dirty. Too many signs in too many colors wanted me to stop, too many state flags used as props, too many arrows pointing me toward too many deals too good to pass. The farther through Amarillo I drove, the more it felt as if I were in a Texas theme park, and not a particularly clean one at that. Nothing about any of the shops or restaurants or buildings along I-40 felt genuine. Hunger be damned, I decided I wasn't stopping in Amarillo.

A truck stop at the western edge of the town advertised a Subway sandwich shop as part of their offerings, so I decided to take them up on it. In this case I wanted something familiar, even maddeningly so. When I took the exit and made my way to the front of the store, I saw a parking lot jammed with all sorts of cars except SUVs, mini-vans, and pickup trucks. Not a Cadillac with steer horn hood ornament in sight.

I stopped, grabbed food and ate quickly, and was on my way within 20 minutes. A stop at the truck stop to fill up the car's tank, and back onto the highway. Shortly after re-entering I-40, I saw a sign: New Mexico – 70 miles. Clouds were beginning to collect overhead, but it didn't matter. I was getting closer to my destination, and in 70 miles I'd be only a state away. Granted, it was a huge state, but still.

An hour later I was in New Mexico. The terrain had changed little by little as I left Amarillo. There were more hills, then more large hills, then what looked to be small peaks and buttes in the distance. I began to see small prickly pear cacti along the roadways, and there was less green to the landscape. Once I hit New Mexico a whole new atmosphere unfolded, dramatically and drastically, within miles of entering the state. Glorious purple and red and gold landscapes of rock and mesas, cliffs cut away by wind and water. The scenery had a serene and lonely feel to it, as if water was a memory and strong wind a constant companion. There were abundant sagebrushes blowing along the highway and across the highway. I had never been there, but it was wildly apparent why the nickname of the state was, "The Land of Enchantment." It was enchanting, and I wanted to look at every sight instead of driving, but that wasn't to be.

After another mile I saw the first sign, a huge, colorful board that would have been right at home in 1956. It was extolling the many wonderful virtues of stopping at Clines Corners, apparently a rest stop/restaurant/gift shop/local oddity/iconic landmark. It was only 60 miles ahead. Until the next sign – or next 2 signs, one on each side of the expressway – let me know it was only 59 miles away. And this was my entertainment for the next hour, looking for and at these signs, each one a bit different, one touting the best pie in the state, the next one letting me know they had authentic Navajo jewelry. There was apparently nothing that Clines Corners didn't have. I would venture a guess that if you needed an oil derrick, a family of pure white guinea pigs, and a hit man who drove a vintage Edsel, it could all be had at Clines Corners. Which really might have been verified by a sign about 20 miles down the road that proclaimed Clines Corners had "Something for Everyone!"

So of course I had to stop. How can you be amused by 60 miles of signage and not stop? Where the size and colors of the signs and surroundings in Amarillo screamed a disingenuousness, these signs screamed a child-like nostalgia, as if they hadn't noticed that it was 2016 now, or if they had they were too embarrassed to do anything about it. Besides, I hadn't taken the time to do much of anything during the trip, at least nothing of a local flavor. This would be a kick.

A blind man would have had a difficult time missing this exit. Literally a sign every 50 yards for the final mile, with huge arrows guiding cars and campers and perhaps small, low-flying aircraft onto the exit and into the parking lot. It sat high on a hill to the north of the highway, and the building, while modest, was as colorful as every one of those signs. Oh, and surrounded by cars and trucks of all shapes and sizes. I parked in back, got out, and spent the next 3 minutes hiking to the front door.

Inside was again as colorful and jovial as the signs. Restaurant in back, complete with soda fountain and seats at the soda counter. Acres of souvenirs and knick-knacks, food items, t-shirts, hats, stuffed lizards. Across from the restaurant was the jewelry store, with large photos of turquoise watches and broaches and bolo ties hung from the ceiling, letting customers know where those goods could be found. Kids were running, squealing in delight, and parents were trying to corral them while not dropping the Clines Corners oven mitts that Aunt Judy back home would love so much. A loudspeaker overhead announced that restaurant seating was ready for guest number 72.

It was a state fair in a box.

I stood there, motionless, taking it all in. When I felt the need to explore this alien place in greater depth, I turned to my right and immediately bumped into someone.

"Oh, jeez, I'm sorry," I said. I looked at her, and saw a woman, perhaps late 20's or early 30's, wavy red hair, and the deepest green eyes I had ever seen in my life. I stopped for a moment, the apologized again. "Really, I'm sorry."

She smiled and said, "Oh, hey, no problem, I'm sorry too, I think I was in a state of shock looking at everything and bumped into you."

"This place is, . . . "

"Yes, it is," she said. "Never seen anything quite like it."

We both stood there nursing an odd and uncomfortable silence, which I finally broke by saying, "Well, again, I'm sorry for, I guess falling into you."

"Oh, don't be sorry," she said, "As much me as you."

I smiled. "Okay then. Have a, . . . have a good browse, or shop."

She laughed. "You too."

I walked away slowly, and much more carefully. After reaching the cavernous t-shirt section, I looked back at where she still stood. She was looking out over the floor, and as she turned her head she saw me again, smiled, and gave me a little wave that either said "have fun" or "good luck with this place." Couldn't tell which one.

I spent the next 25 minutes wandering the extent of their floor, stopping for a chocolate shake, and not buying anything emblazoned with the "Clines Corners" logo or colors. I circumnavigated the part of the store where small twins, no more than 5 years old, were throwing an

Olympic-level tantrum about not being able to buy gummy dinosaurs. I avoided the face-painting area. I saw plenty of people who I recall looked eager upon entering but who now looked tired and equally eager to get back on the road. Not surprisingly, most of those people had kids.

I was about to head out when I almost bumped into my green-eyed female acquaintance from earlier. We both smiled as we passed, and she said, "I don't think I want to be here, but I can't seem to drag myself away yet, either."

"I know," I replied, "like watching a train wreck in slow motion, only more colorful."

She laughed, and continued past. I think that was a sign that it was time for me to get back in my car and make my way to Albuquerque, where I would stop for tonight. I exited, shake in hand, and made the trek back to my car. Ten minutes later I was back on the expressway.

The sixty mile drive to Albuquerque was slowed by a nasty SUV vs. motorcycle accident that brought the westbound lanes to a halt about 20 miles east of town. As we waited, watching the sun ease toward the horizon and cast a golden glow on the buttes and mountains in the distance, I thought again about how different a place I was in, physically and emotionally, than just 48 hours ago. But this time my thoughts tended toward feeling a bit disillusioned, as though I had let people down by being here. Sarah, mom, Elena, Beth, even Dan and some of my other friends – their lives didn't look much different now than they did Monday. Mine was, if not upside down, then at least tumbling, sideways, in flux. What had I done to deserve the chance to start again, go somewhere new? I looked side to side, and saw gorgeous scenery, shapes and colors and ridges and formations that I had never seen before, that many of my friends have never seen before or may never see in their lives. How did I rate all this? I was the one with a failed marriage, an uncertain future, and a displaced mother who didn't want me out here doing any of this. Why did I get to have all the fun and adventure?

I thought of how Sarah and I had always planned on taking a trip to Santa Fe, how the atmosphere was always portrayed as spiritual, relaxed, casual, a perfect getaway for people who want to get in touch with each other outside of a congested, materialistic environment. Magazines and television shows touted the great food there, different magazines waxed poetic about the art galleries, and every picture of Santa Fe returned by a Google search showed a delightfully clean, small city, high in the hills enveloped by an expansive blue sky. What's not to love? Each spring we talked about going there, and each summer for some reason or another we didn't do it.

One year, I think five years ago, I was on the computer researching airfares when Sarah sat down across the table from me. "Okay, so as far as summer vacations might go," she started, "what do you think about Omaha?"

I slowly looked up, then looked side to side, as if there was a hidden camera somewhere recording my response to this obviously outlandish statement. "I try not to think about Omaha, to be honest," I replied. "Why do you ask?"

"Welllll," she dragged out, "I talked to my sister today, . . ."

"Oh good God," and I brought my hands to my forehead.

" . . . . and she was saying that her and Mike were going to be there for a conference he was going to, and that it would be a great time and place for us to get together and spend some time, especially since they haven't been in town for so long."

Sarah's sister, Anne, and her husband Mike, lived in Spokane, Washington. They moved there just before our wedding, when Mike was offered a position on the Mathematics faculty at Gonzaga University. Anne had grown to accept Spokane more than like it, and was always looking for reasons to either travel (particularly in the summer, when Mike was supposed to have more free time) or was secretly searching for other jobs for him or her that would relocate them. But Mike loved Spokane, loved Gonzaga, and took to his position so much that he accepted additional teaching or research spots almost every summer, leaving Anne nothing to do but spend another year in Spokane and hope the next year would be better. This year there was apparently a reason for them to be in Omaha, and sisters being sisters, I guess they thought it would be the perfect time and place for a couple's vacation.

"So, what exactly would we all be doing in Omaha?" I asked. "All I know about it is that it's in Nebraska, and most people tend to find reasons to not go to Nebraska."

"Oh it'll be fun," Sarah said, excitement rising in her voice and expressions. "And besides, it's not so much where you are, it's who you're with."

"Then can we all be together somewhere else? I mean, would they like Santa Fe, maybe they can meet us there on the way home after the conference."

"Oh be serious, they're not going to spend three days in Omaha, then fly again to Santa Fe before flying home, that's not practical." She sat back. "Besides, I already told her it sounded like a great idea and to count us in."

"Uuuuhhhhh . . . really? If you said yes without asking me, then why did you just ask me?"

"Oh come on, it'll be fun, I promise."

"Ya know, I never know what to say or talk about with Mike. He's a nice guy but we really have nothing in common."

"Oh, ask him about his conference, or how his teaching is going, you'll think of something."

"But see, that assumes I'm interested in his conference or teaching math, and I'm not. I find math tedious and dull." I leaned closer, and grabbed her hands across the table. "We've been talking for so, so long about going to Santa Fe, and I thought this was the year it would happen, we both have the time, we have the money, it's all aligned for us."

She pulled her hands away. "You still just don't like my sister, do you," she said, and then stood up and walked away from the table.

And the truth was I wasn't a big fan of Anne. She lived life as though everyone around her was supposed to be equally enthralled with her life as she was, and wherever she went she wanted to be the center of attention. I was always nice to her, was never rude nor obstinate, but Sarah was always certain that I was harboring some deep-seated dislike. I didn't hate her, I didn't even really dislike her; I just felt that, if we hadn't been in-laws, she was not the type of person I would ever have been friends with, and if I had met her someplace else in life, I'm sure I wouldn't have spent more than one minute talking to her. But this was a black and white thing: if you didn't love Anne like Sarah did, then you hated her. No in between.

So I closed the browser window with the airfares, then closed the laptop. Later that night we agreed that we were going to Omaha. We never did get to Santa Fe. The following year, something came up that got in the way, I didn't remember now exactly what, but I do know the idea was shot down almost immediately. Eventually, as our marriage continued to fray and splinter, we manufactured reasons to not go. By the end of our marriage, neither of us were able to say the name of the city without spitting venom as well. It became a yardstick that measured lost dreams and wounded hopes. It was a mythic, phantom trip that left me both angry and resentful. And on top of that, I suddenly became the person who "hated Anne and Mike," and she held that against me, never passing up a chance to take a little dig at me over it. But we all tend to create our own truth when we're wounded. In her eyes, everything I said or thought was anti-Anne, and I could never get the benefit of the doubt, even when saying something positive. My attitude toward her sister was collateral damage.

I do know that shortly before our divorce became final, I received one final, bitter, self-righteous email from Anne, taking me to task for not loving Sarah more, for not trying harder to be a better husband, a better companion, a better man. She made it clear that in her mind I was responsible for what had happened between Sarah and me, and that I deserved all the scorn and unhappiness that she was sure would follow. She finished with what I'm sure she thought was a boast, about how she had once been interested in me but had been able to see what kind of person I really was, and she was so, so happy that she never pursued me. Well, that made two of us. Her email did nothing more than cement in my mind my opinion of her as a spoiled and immature brat, but for some reason the words lingered even when I laughed them off. Whether my subconscious found any truth in her words or if instead my sense of responsibility accepted some of her accusations, the email was long gone, but the tone and words remained. Perhaps I wasn't worthy of anything good.

It was those words, those feelings, that coursed through me as I crawled past the wreckage on the road, hideous twisted metal flanked on both sides by grand purple and crimson landscapes, a strange juxtaposition of anguish and joy, loss and birth. I wanted to experience and fully feel that joy, be part of the colors and flavors that brought life and hope, yet every time I stopped and considered how lucky I was, I fell back into patterns of self-doubt and feeling unworthy. My head was leading me to a great adventure and a new chapter in life; my heart was pumping my veins full of sorrow and guilt.

Just as we started to move at a snail's pace, my phone's text alert beeped. I looked over: another text from Elena.

Seems empty for us to be going out tonight without you here — can you send a life-sized inflatable Wade? Missing you, hope you're missing us too. E

I smiled. I did miss her, miss all my friends back home. Home. What would I call Sedona once I got there, once I'd been living there for a few months, a few years? Would Chicago always be home? Would Elena, Dan, all of them be "my people back home," or would they eventually become "my friends form the old days in Chicago?" It made me miss her a bit more, and I wished she were here, just sitting beside me cracking jokes, talking, telling me that I was a good person, a good guy, looking at me with her blend of friendship and lust. Just one more time.

When the car stopped again, I quickly texted her back a smiley face. She'd know I got her text, know it made me happy, and know I was thinking about her and the people back home – all without needing to type. Emojis are wonderful.

The traffic eventually crawled past the accident, and like magic we were going 75 again, the landscape whipping past. As we climbed to a higher elevation, rounding the Sandia Mountains heading into town, I watched as the readings on my outside temperature gauge started dropping, slowly at first and then in 2 or 3 degree steps. By the time Albuquerque was in sight, the temperature had fallen to 39, quite a bit cooler than the weather I had been enjoying so far. I made a mental note to grab a heavier jacket out of the trunk once I stopped at the hotel.

I exited toward the Uptown area, where I had booked a Hyatt Place for the night. No particular reason, except that it was only two blocks of the highway, near food and entertainment, and Hyatt hotels are usually reliable. I found the place with no trouble, grabbed my jacket and bag, and checked in. Quick elevator to my fourth floor room, opened the door, dropped the bag, flopped onto the feathery plush king-sized bed – and promptly fell asleep.

I awoke perhaps 2 hours later, the darkness of the room interrupted only by the light from the street seeping in through the seams between the drapes. I arose, my back and legs complaining about the time spent curled in the front seat of my car the past three days, and switched on the nearest lamp. Third day driving, third night in a strange place, strange room. Tomorrow would be fourth night in a strange room, but at least it would be in Sedona, and a room that would soon become familiar, soon become home. I had always liked traveling, liked exploring other cities, other places, other cultures, but those were times when I would usually spend multiple nights in the same place. Nothing like this road trip, a new bed every night. There were times I found it hard enough to sleep in my own bed; finding sleep in unfamiliar beds, night after night, was a chore bordering on a challenge, which is why I welcomed the nap, unexpected as it was. Any sleep was welcome. Anyway, my stomach was beckoning. A quick splash of water on the face and neck, a new shirt, and I was ready to find some dinner.

I walked south a block to an entertainment area that featured numerous shops and restaurants. I figured walking was preferable to driving; I'd done plenty of that recently, and again, my body could take a break from the front seat. It was also rather pleasant to get out into some fresh, cool air, as the chill helped waken me. I passed the chain restaurants, wanting again to experience something endemic to Albuquerque, something I wouldn't get in Chicago, Oklahoma City, or even Sedona. Within two blocks I saw it: Fuzzy Puppy Brewpub. Good lord, with a name like that . . . how can it not be wonderful? I had found my food and drink for the night.

Fuzzy Puppy was similar to Tornado Alley Brewery and Grill from the previous night, but had a different, more urban vibe, which I found interesting since I had never considered Albuquerque particularly urban. It was a city, yes, and the largest one in New Mexico. It was also home to University of New Mexico, the largest university in the state. But still - - one never considers New Mexico, in general, to be cosmopolitan or trendy. One expects cowboy boots, brass belt buckles the size of hub caps, and cattle ranchers, not citified yuppies.

I grabbed a seat at the bar, as was my custom, and ordered a pint of the house IPA. The décor leaned toward urban casual, with a side of eclectic chic punctuated by college pride. Yes, there were a couple of big screen TVs in the bar area, but there were also numerous smaller monitors with trivia games, while off to the side of the bar area were two pool tables, a few dart boards, and even an air hockey table. They were apparently ready for any interest from their clientele, and weren't about to lose anyone to disinterest. The people ranged from college kids in branded sweatshirts all the way to a few couple in suits and dresses. Being a Sunday night it wasn't crowded, but there was still a hum to the atmosphere, and while not as loud as Tornado Alley Brewery it certainly wasn't a funeral home either.

The IPA was surprisingly good, and I decided it would pair well with the New York strip steak that was tonight's special, so I ordered that. Again while I waited I spent time just taking in the feel of the place, from the sights and sounds in the bar area to the smells that wafted from the kitchen. Nobody sitting next to me tonight, so no conversations for me to eavesdrop on, which was probably best. I could just let my mind wander without interruption or getting sidetracked.

The food arrived, sizzling on the plate. I dug in, and as I ate I watched the bartender as he continually drifted to the far end of the bar, where his girlfriend (new acquaintance? potential after work hook-up?) sat, and he chatted her up whenever he had a free moment. She was young, probably young enough to be there using an ID with a name and birth date that wasn't hers, and her long blonde hair fell neatly to her exposed shoulders (thanks to the skin-tight sleeveless white dress). She threw her head back and laughed when she was supposed to, and her fingertips traced the rim of her glass of rose as she leaned toward him every time she spoke. I couldn't tell who was the hunter and who was the hunted, but I had the feeling that by midnight it wouldn't matter.

When the steak and fries were gone but some of the beer was left, I draped my jacket over my chair and motioned the bartender over. "Listen, take my plate but not my beer, okay? Just hittin' the restroom, I'll be back in a sec."

"You got it," he replied as he grabbed the plate.

I looked around, and saw the neon sign for the restrooms toward the side of the restaurant, at the other end of the bar. I stepped off the stool, walked along the bar, passed the blonde on the prowl, and turned the corner toward the restroom doors. And for the second time today, ran directly into someone.

She fell to the side, didn't lose her balance but put her arms out and caught herself on the wall. I did the same in the other direction, only I steadied myself on a free-standing ATM, waiting to save me like a squared R2-D2. Simultaneously I tried to reach out to catch her, but she was moving away from me anyway, making my heroics physically impossible.

"Oh geez, I'm so sorry," I said, "I didn't see . . ." I stopped talking and looked at her. Her green eyes and red curls. No fucking way.

She caught her balance and looked at me, and her eyes grew wide when recognition set in. "Oh my god, it's you, from that rest stop" she said.

"Yeah, what are the odds?"

"Okay, wait, are you, like, stalking me here or something?" she asked, and I wasn't sure if she was kidding or not.

"Huh? What, no, no, of course not," I stammered, "I mean, ... no, how would I know, or . . . I mean, . . ."

She laughed. "I'm kidding, I'm kidding. It's just crazy that I bump into you, like literally, twice in one day. That's kinda weird, dontcha think?"

"God yes," I said, "I was, . . well I was really shocked when I realized it was you. I mean, yeah, definitely weird."

We stood there for a couple of uncomfortable seconds until she extended her hand. "Well hi, I'm Leannette."

I took her hand in a gentle shake. "I'm Wade, nice to meet you. That's a very pretty name, not one you hear too often."

"Thank you, I tell people my parents couldn't make a choice so they went with both options," she said. "I've got so many nicknames because of it that I answer to almost anything."

"Handy," I said. "So what are you doing here? I mean, you know, I see you an hour from here in a funky roadside gift shop, now you're here, . . . you live in Albuquerque? Or are you passing through, and of all the places in the city we end up in the same one?" I paused for a second, then said, "Or, waaaaait a minute, maybe you're the one stalking me. Is that the deal?" I punctuated that with a big smile, which she returned.

"Uh, well, long story."

"Yeah, well, so many of them are, and we all have one" I replied. We stood for another second, and I continued. "So, are you here with friends, family, I should probably let you get back, . . ."

"Well see, that's part of the long story," she said. "I was here with people, but they ended up leaving, so right now I'm here alone."

It was then that I noticed she had a coat and small rolling suitcase with her. "I'm sitting over at the bar," I offered, "if you'd like, why don't join me and you can tell me all about your long story, and how you got from that gift shop to here."

She smiled again. "Uhm, . . . okay, that would be nice, thanks."

"I'm over there, the seat with the jacket over it," I pointed, "just gimme a sec, let me go to the washroom, . . ."

"Oh, yeah, yeah, you go, I'll be over there," she said, and started walking toward the bar.

I hurried into the restroom, took care of business, washed up, and quickly went back to my seat at the bar. She was sitting on the stool to my right. "So, Leannette, what's your story," I asked as I climbed into place on my stool, "how did you end up here, in an Albuquerque bar on a

Sunday night?"

"Well, it started, and I don't know how far back you want me to go with this, . . ."

"Oh heck," I said, "start at the beginning, it's early."

She laughed, "Okay then. It started in Minneapolis, which is where I live. Or lived. I got out of a bad relationship about a year ago, and not much of my family is left in that area, so after a while I figured why not go somewhere new, preferably somewhere with sun and sand. So about a month ago I talked to my boss about working remotely, since I'm in corporate training that's something I can do pretty easily, and eventually got that approved, and then signed up for a long-distance ride-share thing, you know, where someone else is driving and they agree to take you with for a fee, usually half the gas, that sort of thing.

"Anyway, I found an older couple that were heading to San Diego, and I thought, 'Perfect, that's about as different from Minneapolis as I can get,' and I made arrangements with them to go along with them on the trip. We left a few days ago and made our way down here. When we bumped into each other earlier at that crazy roadside shop, they had wanted to stop, rest, get some food, some souvenirs for family, that sort of thing. So they were wandering the store when we first met, which is why I was looking kinda maybe lost and out of it, it was kind of disorienting in there after dozing in the backseat for hours."

"I can imagine."

"So then after we left, they got a phone call, I guess their son was in a car accident or something, him and his whole family, and it sounded pretty bad, so as soon as they got to Albuquerque they dropped me off and turned around and headed back to Minnesota."

"Yikes. The son and the family okay?"

"I really don't know, although they both seemed really shaken and upset, I mean, I was even worried about them driving back as upset as they were, but . . ."

"Yeah, something like that happens, you're gonna head back, no questions asked."

"Right," she said. "So they asked if it would be a problem if they dropped me here, well, I mean across the street at the Hampton Inn, they gave me money to cover a hotel and a bus, but other than that," she paused, leaned back opened her arms with her palms up, "here I am, sitting in a strange bar in a strange city with a strange guy." And she smiled. "Well, maybe not as strange a guy as some of them I've seen in the area, but you know, . . ."

"Oh sure, yeah, you don't know me from anyone, just a random guy you bumped into earlier in a remote tchotchke emporium."

"Oh, that's a good phrase for it, I gotta remember that, a remote tchotchke emporium. Maybe even 'an overly colorful remote tchotchke emporium'," and she giggled.

The bartender approached. "Either of you need anything?"

I asked her, "Where were you sitting somewhere before, did I take you away from your table, or your food or something?"

"No, no, I was just walking in," she replied, then turned to the bartender. "Could I please have a, hmmm . . . do you have a good Cabernet by the glass?"

"Our house wine's Sterling, let me give you a taster to make sure you like it."

"Great," she said, and he left to retrieve her sip. She then turned back to me. "Okay, that's how I'm here, and why, now what about you? Albuquerque your home?"

"Oh, heck no," I replied, and gave her the shortened version of my decision to leave after my bad relationship, and about my need to distance myself from my past, starting geographically. During the story the bartender delivered her taster; she liked it, and he brought a full glass, which she sipped as we spoke.

"I can understand heading west and starting fresh," she said. "I mean, that's in a way what I'm doing, trying to start over somewhere new, somewhere different, somewhere where I won't be reminded of yesterday around every corner. Anyway, so why Sedona?"

"Means 'peace,' an' I figured I could use some peace in my life, . . . seen enough and heard enough of the place, figured, what the hell, let's give it a shot."

"Hey, why not," she said, "you have to take chances, try new things, see what's out there. No fun to do the same thing all the time, or make the same mistakes all over again."

"Exactly," I said, "and ya know, some of my friends back home, they get it, and some of them really don't, they think it's just running away from life. Especially my mom, she really doesn't get it."

"Well sure, moms won't, but the others, unless they've gone through something as all-encompassingly devastating like a divorce, or the death of a spouse or partner or something like that, they'll never get it. And to them, all you can do is thank them for their concern and do what's right for you."

"And that's why I'm here," I replied. "You can't make everyone happy, and trying to do so will make you crazy. I think . . . no, I know, it made me crazy."

"God knows it can, especially if you're not paying attention," she said. The bartender again approached, but before he could say anything she turned and asked, "Can I get a menu please?"

"Sure, let me grab one."

"Oh, I'm sorry," I said, "you must be hungry and I didn't even offer, . ."

"Oh stop," she said, "I'm hungry, not some starving refugee."

"Yeah, but I should have, . ."

The bartender returned with the menu before I could finish. She took it from him and quickly scanned it as he waited. After a quick 10 seconds she said, "Can I have the steak fajitas, please? With guacamole on the side?"

"Coming up," he said, and took the menu and headed to place the order.

She turned to me again. "And will you help me eat it all?"

"I would be a cad to turn down a stranded damsel in distress."

"Oh, is that what you think of me after hearing my story, a damsel in distress?" Her hands went to her hips, and she lowered her head to look at me from the tops of her eyes. When I didn't reply she started laughing. "I'm yanking your chain, relax," she said. "I know, just a figure of speech, I get it."

I exhaled. "Good. Last thing I want to do is insult someone I've just met." I took a sip of my beer – a big sip, drained the glass. "I just, . . .I mean, I hope you know I meant that as a figure of speech, nothing more than that."

"Oh relax, not offended," she said. "Actually kinda cute and chivalrous. Hard to find that anymore."

I smiled. "Okay. Well, okay. So," I said changing the direction of the conversation, "Now this may sound stupid, but why is it that, in a strange, unfamiliar city, you can find someone to talk to like a long lost friend, and even at that, how come you're not shying away from me like I'm some strange stalker or creepy bar guy? I mean, I would think, female, alone in a city she doesn't know, that doesn't seem like a place where you start trusting every person who talks to you. Ya know what I mean, or am I way off?"

She leaned closer. "Are you saying there's a reason why I shouldn't be here, out alone, talking to people, . . . or you in particular?"

"No, really, I just was wondering, . . ."

"How safe it is in general for me, out just wandering on a Sunday night, talking to guys, or one guy, I don't know? Well, no more or less safe than if I was doing it at home, I guess. I mean, sure, back home I'm in a familiar setting, a familiar bar in my neighborhood, but once you strip that away, sitting alone in any bar, familiar or not, it's a crapshoot as to who you might meet. There are creeps everywhere, and there are good people everywhere. You just gotta develop that sense of who's who, and learn to trust your instincts."

"Okay, that makes sense. Never thought of it that way. Me, I come into an unfamiliar city, unfamiliar bar or restaurant, I tend to not talk to people, keep to myself, just see what the place and people are like. I'm not real talkative with people I don't know."

"But then there's me."

"Yeah, there's you, and that's not the norm for me. Well, bumping into someone twice in one day, in two different locations, definitely a new one, but still, I'm not sure I'd normally end up sitting here with you talking." I paused. "And I can't quite figure out why it's so easy for me to be doing it now, so see, that's the thing, I don't know if this is easy and normal or odd and unusual, us meeting and sitting here eating and drinking like this."

She sipped her wine again. "I think it was meant to be," she said, "I mean, why on earth, how on earth, would two people from different places like you say bump into each other twice on the same day but in two different places? Must be a reason, fate, kismet, . . . not sure." She slowed down her talking and looked more closely at me. "But I do think there's something, somewhere, 'out there'," and she looked up and around, and held her arms out with palms up, "there's a reason we met, and there's a reason we're here. And that's why I have no doubt you're not a stalker or creepy bar guy, karma wouldn't do that to me. Or to us." She smiled. "And again, my highly developed spidey-sense tells me you're one of the good guys."

Her words were the perfect segue to a sizzling plate of steak fajitas being delivered in front of her. The smell filled the air, and despite my earlier dinner I was suddenly hungry again. She shuffled all of the foods around for ease of access: steak in front, warm tortillas between us, guacamole to her right (since I declined any), and the rest of the toppings a short reach above the main course. Serving plates, utensils and napkins in place, we dove in.

I ate sparingly, letting her take most of the food. We made small talk between bites – music, movies, a bit about our families – but mostly we ate, or I watched as she ate. She was . . . well, unexpected, of course, but also rather refreshing. She wasn't someone from my past, or related to my past, or with some knowledge of my past. She also wasn't someone from "my life" – nobody from work, from my industry, nobody with ties or relations to Chicago or Geneva or anywhere I've been or anyone I've touched. Everything we talked about – her, me – it was all new, all from scratch. Like stumbling upon a new author that you've never heard of, and it's surprisingly good and comfortable.

And she was – well, not a classic beauty in the Grace Kelly or Scarlett Johansson sense, but very much a study in bubbly/cute/pretty. She smiled with ease and it lit up her face, and her eyes would sparkle, and her laugh was easy and infectious. At this point she had her long red curls tied into a pony tail flipped over her right shoulder, and her nails were playfully colored, each one striped like the flag of Jamaica, making them flash like rainbows as she ate her food. In some ways, the classic "girl next door," as long as the girl next door had spirit and humor and an intoxicating smile.

That was one argument that occurred regularly between Sarah and myself. She was always fretting about her looks and her weight – two pounds over what she wanted, didn't like her arms in the mirror, afraid any given pair of jeans would make her behind look big. I was always telling her that I thought she looked great – primarily because I usually did think that. She would put on a dress for an event, put her hair up, and she'd turn heads. But she was always so insecure – I half believed that body issue insecurity was a normal female trait, so often I waved it off. But it got bad enough that she became obsessive about it, to the point where it became a distraction between us.

I worked out, or at least tried to, maybe 3-4 times a week. When Sarah had to lose weight – or inches, or fit into an item of clothing – she made it an obsessive point to work out every day, sometimes twice a day.

Eating patterns would follow the same vein: salads, yogurt, quinoa all became sudden staples of our diet when she had body issues. And if she was eating it, I was eating it, because as she said, "It's disrespectful to eat fattening food when your wife is trying to lose weight. And it's mean spirited as well."

Which would be fine for a few days, but damn it, I'm a burger and pizza and barbeque guy, and no salad is going to hold me for weeks on end. "Me not eating the exact same as you isn't disrespectful," I'd say, "it's more disrespectful for you to force upon me the same standards as you force upon yourself. Me topping a salad with steak is not me telling you I want you to fail."

"Well it's not helping me either, and as my husband you're supposed to be helping me, not working against me. Tempting me is working against me, even worse, conspiring against me."

So yes, my desire for a cheeseburger was a great conspiracy against her getting into a size 4 pair of skinny jeans. What was unfortunate is that this behavior started maybe two years into our marriage, and I'm not really sure what precipitated it. She was never heavy, never even close to it, nor were her parents or her sister. She looked stunning at her 10-year High School reunion with little effort. I'd seen pictures of her growing up, and she was an adorably thin girl, and even in high school she was what any person would call "just right." Why can some people be "just right" but not picture themselves, or think of themselves, as "just right?" Why do some people's default setting immediately veer toward "I'm somehow broken, or not good enough?"

I was pulled out of my thoughts by someone saying "Hey." I looked and it was Leannette, looking at me while holding a tortilla filled with steak and sour cream and salsa out towards me.

"Oh, sorry, . ."

She moved the fajita toward my mouth. "Open up." I opened my mouth, and she fed me the end of the fajita. I bit, taking some in my mouth and allowing her to move the rest away before any dripped on the counter or our clothing. "Thank you," I said, or tried to say through my mouthful, but it came out more as ""Fangrew."

"You said you'd help eat this, remember? Gotta hold up your end of the bargain." She took a bite from the half fajita she was still holding, the moved to feed me the last bite. I quickly chewed to open up space, and took in the final bit, nodding and smiling in approval and thanks.

"So," she said after finishing her bite, "if we're sharing food, and if I'm actually hand-feeding you, I get to know more about you." She paused to wipe the corners of her mouth with her napkin. "So your marriage, or divorce, what happened? How did you go from happily married to divorced and moving across country?"

"Like anything, it happened both gradually and suddenly," I said after a moment of thought. "Sarah and I, that's her name, Sarah, . . ."

"Yeah, could've guessed that."

". . . yeah, okay, so Sarah and I started out, we were pretty young, early 20s, and we met and it just sorta clicked, I guess you'd say. The longer we were together it seemed like we were really in sync with each other, wanted the same things in life, compatible, same tastes and likes in a lot of the day-to-day things that drive life."

"Like what," she asked.

"Well," I sighed, and thought for a second, "at first, just that stuff on the surface, you know, liked the same movies, similar music, same sort of activities, neither of us were big drinkers, we didn't hang out with friends at bars all the time, that sort of thing. We both had, at least I thought we both had, the same general outlook on life, the same beliefs, same political and social leanings. Both wanting life to be simple, have jobs we liked, settle down in a nice place, live a decent life. Typical suburban American Dream." I paused again, then laughed. "Oh, and we both liked dogs, so we had a beagle."

"Oh how cute! What was his or her name?"

"Watson. It fit him perfectly. He's with her now."

"Ohhh," and she made a cute sad frowny face.

"Anyway, we just, . . .we just fit, ya know? I never worried about being anything other than myself, and I was comfortable around her to just be me.

"At least, I thought I was. As time went on, and we grew older, we seemed to develop these quirks, I mean both of us, and it seemed like these quirks get like slivers under your skin, they start so small, and then there are more and more, from both of us, and pretty soon we're . . ." And I stopped for a moment.

"Pretty soon you're what," Leannette asked?

"I think there were more quirks, or more slivers, that affected me, and I let that show in my behavior more than her. I think, being truthful, Sarah was willing to ride it out and hope things would go back to the way they were, but there, ... there were more things I think that I learned about me, and that made some of the issues between us larger and more difficult for me to look past.

"Like, I think, or I can see, how I became kinda passive-aggressive, we'd be bickering about something, probably something stupid, . . . oh yea, like our bedroom, she wanted to do this wallpaper on all the walls and I thought that was too much, but she was so insistent and inflexible about it that I just said fine, do all four walls, an' I said it just to get the argument over with and keep things peaceful. Things like that, I'd give in just to keep the peace, and I think a lot of that built up over the years."

"Oh God, you were being Mister Super-Nice Guy," she said, "happy wife, happy life, right?" She was smiling as she said this, so I was hoping she was saying it in a lighthearted spirit.

"I'm not sure it's 'mister nice guy' any more than it's 'mister doesn't want to fight and create conflict'. I mean, I'm not like that with other people, just her, and I think part of it was her quirks that started getting to me, and I just thought that if she were happier with me and with us, then maybe she wouldn't be so unhappy with herself. It was really about me trying to avoid conflict between us.

"And even now just talking about this, I can see how I really think she was unhappy, even though she always put on a happy face. I mean her parents were like that, always a smile even if it had to mask anger, maybe that's how she was raised, that was what they did, never any signs of conflict. I know I was unhappy, and I have no idea how anyone going through what we were going through could be happy, really happy, ya know? I mean, it just doesn't work that way, walking around people in order not to talk to them, that's not the behavior of happy people, and that's what, . . . well, that's what I was like, but I can't imagine, I know she was aware of it and could see it, I can't imagine that made her happy."

Leannette said, "But what if she was holding out hope that the happiness was still there, just out of reach, and she didn't want to give up on it? Maybe she was unhappy, but not to the point of throwing in the towel. I mean, she married you, you guys must've been in love, at least at one time. Sounds like she just was afraid to give up, or afraid to admit that it was time to give up."

I nodded. "Yeah, that sounds like something she'd do. Although, really by the last year of our marriage, she was such a pessimist, so negative about everything, and that made me nuts too, I used to say she was spending all her time searching behind all the silver linings for a dark cloud. That, and the negativity, that was, well that was one of the quirks, maybe the biggest sliver to me. I mean," and I leaned toward Leannette, "I like life, I want to explore places, do things, I don't want to be afraid of life and what's out there, ya know? Like this, moving across country to someplace I've never been, Sarah would never in a million years do something like that. And, here's another example, I had a job offer about 6 years ago in Seattle, and I thought it would've been a really great job, good opportunity, good company, and she said there was no way she was moving to Seattle, and that if I took the job I was going there by myself, end of story. Wouldn't even consider it. And when I kept asking why, she said it was too far from family, which would've not been the truth about a year later, plus she said it was too rainy and too gray and cool, but she's never been there, she's never visited, and when I said we should go out there to check it out before I accepted any offer, she wouldn't even do that. Nope, she was staying where she was. And that's the sort of thing, I like new things, I like peeking under the covers of life and seeing what night be there. The unknown isn't scary to me, it's interesting, it's fun.

"So in a lot of ways, I stopped pressing things, stopped trying to have fun or try new things, not because it made her unhappy, which it did, but because the conflict and anger was more troubling to me than her unhappiness. I'd rather have the silence than the yelling. So I withdrew, she withdrew, and we found ourselves on different paths."

"So it's just a case of you growing in one direction, and her growing in another, sounds like to me," she said. "I understand that, that happened to my parents, at least that's what I think happened and that's what they've always told me, and that's happened to friends, and in a way that happened with me and Dave, even though we were just living together and not married."

"Ah, yes, you," I said, "we've gotten my uncoupling out of the way, let's hear about yours, the reason you ended up in Albuquerque on a Sunday night in October."

"Fair enough," she said. "So I met Dave about 4 years ago, we worked together, I was this fairly young, new person in the training department, and he was this financial planner."

"Where did you work?" I interjected.

"Ameriprise, a huge financial company in downtown Minneapolis.

Anyway, we met there, started seeing each other, eventually moved in together. And like any new couple things were great, everything was wonderful, you know, glitter and fairies and love songs playing, all that stuff. So after a while when things settle down and we get into our routine of us being us, you start kinda seeing the things you keep hidden from the other one at first, like, he's really type-A work driven, to the point of working a lot of nights and weekends, which he wasn't doing when we started out.

"And to be fair, I love animals, and I volunteered at the local shelter, helping take care of stray and lost and unwanted dogs and cats, that sort of thing."

"That's cool," I said.

"Well yeah, I loved it. But see, his times when he wasn't working started not aligning with my times I wasn't at the shelter, so that became friction, and his view was that his was for his job, so that was more important than my, what he called 'Mother Teresa Act' for the pets, so that wasn't too cool, and then things just started going along like that.

"And even at that, there were times when it would get better, schedules would be in sync, or we'd take a week off and go to Cancun or something, and things would get better and seem more hopeful. And then it wouldn't again."

"And that's when things start to fray," I said, "and it's easy to see that things may not work like we hoped."

"Oh, it was more than that, actually," she said, then she took the final sip form her wine. "No, what really kinda killed it was when I thought I'd surprise him at home instead of going to my shift at the shelter, and walked in on him in bed with another woman from the office. That was kinda the relationship killer in this case."

"Oh good God, yeah, I can see where that would do it," I said. "Geez, someone from right there at work? That's slimy. Someone you knew?"

"No, I wasn't working there by that time. Still, I wanted to kick her in the face and set his balls on fire, but all I could do at that moment was stare and then walk away. You do not expect to walk in on something like that with someone you love, or think you love, or someone you think loves you.

"So I grabbed as much of my stuff as I could and went to my mom's house. The next day when he was at work I went back and cleaned out all of my stuff, including any food I had in the fridge, and left the key stuck in the butter. Fuck him. And that was about eight months ago." She tilted her head and threw back her pony tail. "And here I am, having dinner in Albuquerque, New Mexico with someone I bumped into a few hours ago, on my way to San Diego. At least, I think I'm still on my way there. Gotta get that part figured out still."

"Wow," I said. "Okay, the end of your bad relationship is worse than mine, you win that one."

She laughed. "That's not something I want to win, or wanted to win. But at least I did learn something. Make sure your values are in line with your significant other's values. What comes first in life, what you believe in, how you treat people, and animals for that matter . . . liking the same things, the same food, music, movies, that's fine, but if you view a relationship as something important and meaningful and the other person doesn't, then you two aren't going to be together for very long. Oh, and respect – if you don't respect the other person, who they are, what they believe, then it's over. Or it's not worth keeping."

"Very true," I said, "but at least you're moving forward. I mean, from here it looks like you're moving forward, although I can imagine there were plenty of bad days and nights to get to this place, I'm sure."

The bartender stopped by. "Still working on it?" he asked.

"Nope, I'm done," Leannette said, and she looked at me, "what about you? Still picking, or done?"

"God no, definitely done," I replied.

"Then let me take that out of the way," the bartender said, and he gathered the plates. "Another drink?"

Leannette and I looked at each other for a second, and after a subtle frown from me she replied "No, I think we're done."

"Okay, let me take care of this and get the checks," and he turned and carried the stacked pile of plates away.

I sat back at looked at her as she re-situated herself on her seat and smoothed her hair back. She was . . . different, and different in a good way. She was smart, clever, funny, intelligent, well spoken, she was living life head-on through a bad situation, and the burp in her plans didn't seem to cause any disillusionment. She was stronger, I thought, than most women I had met or had known, but her strength seemed to be the result of her trials and errors, and then learning from life and consolidating it all into her sense of self-confidence. She offered no excuses for what she did, nor apologies for who she was. She was . . .

97

authentic. And damn comfortable with it. I could learn a lot from her.

"So what next," I asked, "where are you going from here?"

"Good question," she answered. "What time is it?"

I pulled out my phone and took a look. "8:33. Why, you have a curfew?"

She playfully slapped my arm. "No. Just wanted to know. Getting my bearing on the whole 'what's next' thing."

"Where are you staying tonight?"

"Still need to figure that out as well," she said. "I think there are a few places right around here, I know if nothing else there's that Hampton across the street where they dropped me. I'm pretty sure one of them will have a room available."

I spoke without thinking. "Okay, listen, I know we just met and all, but I have a room at a hotel maybe a block from here, there's a separate bedroom and a pullout couch in the sitting area, if you'd like, . . ."

"Wow, trying to get me back to your place after only a couple of hours, huh, you move fast for a divorced guy." When I didn't reply she broke into a big grin and said, "No, really, I'm kidding, I can tell that's not you, I'm just giving you a hard time."

"Good, because that's exactly not what I was meaning or going for, that's not my intent, . . ."

"No, I know it's not, and that's sweet that you want to put me up on your couch for the night, and I appreciate it."

"Well no, I was going to offer you the bedroom and I'd take the foldaway, that way you could lock me out and feel safer if you felt the need."

She looked at me, squarely in the eyes, for 10 seconds that seemed like an hour. Her face registered a few expressions: deep thought first, followed by a look that said 'maybe I shouldn't be so trusting,' followed by a gradual smile and warmth that shone from her eyes that was as genuine as I'd seen in ages. "Mama would die a thousand deaths if she heard me say yes or knew what I was doing, but yes, thank you, I would appreciate the kindness of your offer of a place to sleep tonight very much." And with that she leaned over and gave me a petite kiss on the cheek.

"And I don't think I'll be worrying about locking the door. I feel like I know you enough, and know the kind of person you are, that you're not 'one of those guys' and for what it's worth, from all this tonight I feel very comfortable and very safe with you. Comfortable and safe enough to have been here for a few hours and shared not only my fajitas, which ask any of my friends, that doesn't happen often, buy also shared me, my stories, who I am." She put her hand on mine as it rested on the bar. "All night I've been getting very good vibes and good feelings about you, Wade . . . . Wade what? We did first names, I don't know your last name. Oh god, it's not Wade Manson is it? Or, oh God, it's not Wade Trump? Please tell me you're not a Trump."

I laughed. "No, not a Trump, thank god, and not a Manson, not a Hitler, nothing nefarious or evil. Benthagen, Wade Benthagen."

"Benthagen, I like that. Nordic, right?"

"Well done. All grandparents from either Norway or Denmark, although I'm told I have some Pennsylvania Dutch in me from somewhere." I leaned back to take an exaggerated view of her. "And your last name? Let's see, red hair, green eyes, fair complexion, . . . I'm guessing Leannette Yokohama? Or maybe Gonzalez, that's it, isn't it, Leannette Gonzalez."

She laughed. "Oh yeah, anyone can tell I'm from Columbia, daughter of a drug cartel kingpin." She wiped at an eye. "Really, would you be very surprised if I said my last name was Shaughnessy? One hundred percent Irish, father's side from Dublin, mother's from Wexford, down on the southeast coast. Irish girl through and through."

"Yeah, kinda thought you were Irish, but stranger things have happened, so no assumptions. Well, nice to meet all of you, Leannette Shaughnessy."

"Same to you, Wade Benthagen." And we shook hands again, this time our hands lingering for a few seconds. When we broke away, she said, "So it's still fairly early, where do you want to go from here? Want to get another drink somewhere else?"

"Sure, that sounds fine," I replied. "I'm not sure of what else is around here, but there must be someplace else to get a drink in this area, it's all set up as a shopping and eating destination."

"Yeah, that's why I had my ride drop me off here, the map said there were a lot of restaurants and hotels and stuff in this area so I figured I'd be okay."

"Well ya know, we could even walk back to my hotel, it's just a couple of blocks, drop off your bag so you're not carting around all over the place, that way you won't lose it or forget it or anything, . . ."

"Oh, that would be great."

". . . yeah, and then maybe if we see someplace on the way back we can go back to it, or if not maybe walk the other direction and see what's there."

"Sounds like a plan," she replied. "All we need now is, . . ."

And before she could say it, the bartender appeared with two checks. "I'm assuming these were separate?" And he set the checks down in front of us. I reached out to grab both of them, and she did the same. She was quicker.

"Wait, no," I said, "you've been kinda abandoned here, let me get your dinner for you."

"No way, besides, you're letting me stay with you, so I should be paying for your dinner." She turned away from me with both checks, not letting me see them and shielding me from trying to snatch them away.

"Are you sure? Okay, if you won't let me pay for you, at least let me pay my own."

"Nope," she said, "dinner's on me, hotel's on you."

I sighed. "Fine. But next place, I buy the drinks."

"We'll see," she said with a devilish smile, "we'll see about that." She took out a credit card and motioned the bartender back over. When he was near she held out the card and both slips of paper. "I'm paying for both," she said.

"Be right back," he said as he took the items from her hand and turned away.

That done, she sat back and turned and looked toward me. "So, what else do I need to know about you that you haven't told me yet," she asked. "Nobody's life is so uneventful that they can tell their whole life story in two hours, so what else? What other dirt is there about you, what other stories, skeletons in closets." She leaned closer. "Police record? Former boy band member? You didn't invent, like, Instagram or something like that did you, and you're this unassuming millionaire just hanging out in New Mexico." She punctuated all that with a huge smile and flip of the pony tail. "What deep, dark secrets are you hiding?"

"Oh, jeez," I said slowly, "you want skeletons? God, how much time do you have?"

"Oh this sounds good," she said, "for good skeletons I'll make time, we can have all night if the dirt is juicy."

Luckily the bartender returned. He placed a single slip in front of her, along with her card. "I combined the bills so it would be easier," he said.

"Oh great, thank you," she replied, and she grabbed the pen and quickly signed the top copy.

He took that copy and then pen, and said "Thanks guys, have a great night."

"Oh, wait," I said before he walked off, "can I ask, we're both not from around here, if we wanted to go for a nightcap somewhere in walking distance, what would you suggest?"

"Good thinking," Leannette said under her breath.

"Hmm, let's see," he said, "I'd try maybe the St. Francis, . . ."

"Perfect for a Sunday," Leannette chimed in quickly.

" . . . yeah, that would be perfect, but the St. Francis, that's a decent place, they have the trivia games, stuff like that, it's a block east of here, I think on Sundays they're open til 11:00."

"That'll work perfect," I said. "Thanks."

"No problem," he replied, "you guys have a good night." And he walked away.

"To the St. Francis," I said.

"Let's," she said. "Do you still want to drop off my bag first?"

"Yeah, still seems smart, and it's not far, maybe 5 minutes, we have time." I stood and put on my jacket. She did the same and grabbed her bag. "Okay, you good? Let's head out," I said. And we walked out into the night.

We made the quick walk to the hotel. She stopped in the ladies room near the front desk while I went up to the room and dropped off her bag (and straightened up a bit). After I came down we got directions to the St. Francis from the girl at the front desk, and in less than 5 minutes we were there. From the street it was modern and glossy and chic, but the décor inside was warm and comfortable without being too futuristic or pretentious. Being late on a Sunday night the crowd was sparse, so we grabbed a couch in the lounge area and plopped down. The waitress serving the lounge saw us and was there with a drinks menu before we could get comfy.

"Hi there, I'm Angie, I'll be taking care of you tonight, here's our drinks menu, and it's happy hour right now until close." She smiled like a professional and waited patiently while we scanned the menu.

"Ladies first," I said, and waited for Leannette to order something.

"I'm still deciding, so if you know what you want, go ahead."

Angie turned toward me. "Sir?"

"Do you have Woodford Reserve bourbon?"

"Yes, we do."

"Great, Woodford on the rocks, please."

"Okay. And you miss?"

Leannette, still studying the menu, looked up. "I think I'll go simple, vodka and cranberry juice, please."

"Do you want plain vodka or a flavored vodka," Angie the waitress asked?

"Oooh, do you have Absolut Kurant?"

"We do," replied Angie, "have you ever tried it with Absolut Hibiscus? It's amazing!"

"Oh, that sounds interesting," Leannette replied, "let me try that."

"Great, I'll be right back," and she turned and hurried back to the bar. Meanwhile I settled back into the deceptively comfortable and plush couch, into which I was slowly sinking. I looked over and Leannette was doing the same, settling in while trying not to be swallowed whole by the cushions. I let out a small chuckle in her direction.

"What?" She looked at me.

"We're sinking. We may never get out," I said. I tried to sit up and turn toward her, and it almost worked. Instead I was just sinking to the side instead of straight in.

Angie brought our drinks. We took them, then fell back into the soft embrace of the rich upholstery. A quick 'clink' of the glasses and we each took a sip.

"Good?" I asked.

"Mmmm, oh yeah, this is really, really nice," she replied. "Here, try it."

"I'm not much of a hibiscus guy," I said, trying to decline.

"Oh don't be a baby, try something new."

"Okay then," I said, and I leaned over as she held the glass to my lips and gently poured a sip. I swallowed. "Not bad," I said, "I'm not big on vodka, and not big on flowery drinks, but that's not bad at all."

"See," she said, "you try something new, never know what you might like."

"God, you sound like my mom when I was little, trying to get me to eat Brussels sprouts or something."

"And did you ever try them?"

"Eventually."

"And did you like them?"

"Well, eventually, yes, so . . ."

"So your mother and I are right, try new things, you never know when your new favorite is out there waiting for you."

"Hey, I try new things," I said, "Hell, this whole driving cross country to someplace new, that's a real new thing, that's bigger than Brussels sprouts or vodka."

"True," she replied, "but ya gotta take little steps too, not just big steps. Sometimes a thousand little steps will get you father than one big step. And besides," she said, leaning closer into me, "little steps can be fun. That's how you find all the cool things in life. Anyhow, I'd bet if you'd never tried Brussels sprouts you'd never have decided to try something as huge as moving cross country. Little steps prep you for bigger steps." She looked at me and took another sip of her drink. Then she leaned forward suddenly, a curious expression on her face.

"Hey wait, skeletons, we're supposed to be talking about skeletons," she said, and she poked a finger into my side. "You were going to spill on all the things in your life that you haven't spilled yet." She sat back, but twisted her body so she was facing me. "So spill."

"Well, like what, exactly? Not sure where to start. Just throw a dart at the wall of my life and see where it lands, or what?" And I leaned toward her and smiled. "And remember, I spill, you spill."

"Fine, fine," she said. "Okay, hmmm . . . .how about high school. Were you a brain, a dork, a burnout? What sort of things and activities were you into in high school? Who was you high school sweetheart? Or your best friend? Oh, oh, did you go to your reunion?"

Wow. Second time in three nights that high school made its way back into my consciousness. "Uhm, okay," I slowly replied, "let's see, . . .

"High School." Breath. "Little school in suburban Chicago, town called Geneva, we had about 1200 kids in the school. I was, well, not really a brain, although I did get good grades, . . ."

"Not surprised."

"But I wasn't one of those kids that everyone looked at and said, 'oh he's going to Harvard someday,' I was just standard-grade smart, not exceptional smart. And I was into music real big, I played in a band back then."

"Of course, all guys do in high school. Were you the lead guitarist with little high school groupies throwing themselves at your feet?" She giggled.

"No, no, I was the bass player, the guy standing in back. Bass players never got the girls."

"Oh I bet that's not true. Did you have a girlfriend back then?"

"I did," I paused for a moment, "but I'm really not sure I want to get into that right now, if that's okay."

"Sorry, that a sore spot? That your ex, what's her name, . . . Sarah?"

"No, just, . . . well, I'd just rather skip over that right now."

"Oh," she said, sounding a bit taken aback, "Oh, okay, no problem. What about college? Where did you go to college?"

"Miami of Ohio," I said, "double major in English and Marketing. I was really into writing at a young age, you know, . . . the kid sitting at home in the corner on rainy days writing stories, . . . and I kept that up through high school, I wrote for the school paper, the yearbook, and then I thought about being a writer 'for real' so I majored in English. Then I glommed onto Marketing, thinking I could use my writing in advertising, you know, more job possibilities. Did all the typical college stuff, did not join a fraternity, went to all the college hockey games because Miami always had a great team, and generally had a good but not great four years.

"Got out, went back to Chicago, found a job as an ad writer, met Sarah, got married, didn't have kids, got divorced, left Chicago, drove to New Mexico, and met you." I looked at her. "Having a hard time just coming up with skeletons, I guess. I mean, pulling them out of a hat from the past. I'd probably be a boring Google search."

She laughed. "Well, you and me both, I've not exactly led a life of adventure on the front pages of tabloids either."

"I find that hard to believe."

"Seriously, I'm just a Midwest girl from St. Paul, lived in the older part of the city near a couple of colleges, and I was an art geek in school, Art Club and all, painting sets for plays, that sort of thing. Stayed in town for college, University of Minnesota, got a degree in Art Education, spent my college years trying every new thing that came along including more than a few varieties of pot, had boyfriends but no great loves, then graduated and stayed in Minneapolis when I found a job there. Easy-peasy."

"No felonies, not on any international watch list or anything, Interpol not going to bust in and nab you."

"Nope," she said, "just always done my thing and enjoyed what life has brought. At least, that's what I've always tried to do, enjoy life, every day. I had a poster on my wall through high school and college, it said 'Celebrate Life Every Day' and I've tried to do that and live my life that way. Well, be smart about it, of course, but just try to be happy."

"Being happy is a good, noble, and often difficult goal."

"No shit." She took a sip of her drink. "And I get that life isn't one big party, that not every moment is happy and joyful, but damn, you at least need to look for the joy and happiness in life, you have to be open to it, and not feel bad when it happens. I mean, what's the point of life if you're not happy? What kind of life is that?"

"Couldn't agree more," I said, "I think in Buddhist tradition or teachings, whatever, they talk about four noble truths, and it's about how suffering is a part of life, but the goal of life is to remove the suffering and find happiness, and I think that's what a lot of people don't get, that they can be happy if they want, but they have to want it and make it happen, happiness doesn't just happen to you. You have to create your own happiness."

She leaned closer. "Exactly! That's the point, and that's what makes me so crazy sometimes, when people sit back and do nothing and then moan, 'Oh, I'm not happy, this isn't happening, that hasn't happened, oh woe is me,' that sort of crap. If you want to be happy, then find ways to be happy."

"So then," I asked, "right now, at this point in your life, are you happy? Better yet, what makes you happy? What are you looking for in life that will make you happy?"

She sat silent for a moment, an expression on her face as if this were a Mensa-level brain-teaser, then said, "I want to do something that matters, in the big picture you know, not selling cigarettes or teaching insurance professionals how to use some claims software, and I want to be in a place that feels inclusive of people with all ideas, all types of people, and a place that has character and spirituality to it, either in how they treat their people or how the people react to the place, and then I want to be with someone who respects me, makes me laugh, has the same values, same needs, same outlook as me."

"The perfect guy," I said.

"Right, and if he can be great in bed, that's a plus," she said with a laugh. "Okay, what about you, what do you want your life to be so it includes maximum happiness?"

"Well, environment is big for me, I need to be someplace where I can be part of the outdoors, part of nature, feel a part of where I am. And I need, or want, to create, or write, things or something that touches people, but not just makes people feel good or happy, but I want to write something that people will read and think, 'Wow, I'm not alone in how I feel, that sums up how I feel perfectly and someone else feels that too so I must not only not be alone, I must be okay,' you know, something that exposes an emotion or emotional place where people are sometimes afraid to go or acknowledge, but we all have it, and we're all okay."

"Wow," she said, "that's really cool. I wish I could find words that would make an impact on people like that."

"Well I haven't found them yet, but I'm trying. In the meantime, I can sell you some toothpaste, if you like."

She laughed out loud. "Ha ha, God no," she said, "I'll wait for deeper writings than that."

"Fair enough," I said. "And then to top it all off, what person will make me happy? I really don't know. I thought I did, but now I'm not sure I do, and part of that is because I'm not sure that I'm not somehow, maybe subconsciously, finding ways to prevent myself from being happy."

"What do you mean by that?"

"Well, like me and Sarah, when I became unhappy, I became passive-aggressive, and that got in the way of us being happy."

"But no no no," she jumped in, "you just said 'got in the way of *us* being happy,' and that's not what I asked, it's not about an 'us' it's about you. It's like," and she paused, thinking of the right words to say, "it's like, say a couple is a house, each individual person is part of the foundation of the house. You can't build a strong house on a foundation that's weak, each person individually needs to be happy and find happiness before they can be happy as a couple. Bad foundation, the house falls. Not a happy person, hard to build a happy relationship or marriage."

And I sat there, knowing that what she had just said was the perfect analogy for my marriage, and for what happened. I could immediately see, as if a film loop was playing in my mind, so many instances of my wanting to be happy and blaming Sarah on my unhappiness, or putting the responsibility on her. We may have gone into the marriage as equals, with equal parts give and take, but by the end I was taking more than I was giving, and I was always expecting more. I let myself quietly and submissively accept my own unhappiness, and I placed the blame on Sarah. And then I felt bad about it. It was a vicious, crappy circle.

My thoughts were broken by Leannette's hand on mine. "Hey, you okay? You suddenly seemed pretty lost there."

"Just thinking about how completely and totally right you were, you are. The foundation, the house . . . that was me, us, I mean, . . . that was spot-on how we were, and how I was."

"It's human," she said, "remember, like the stories you want to write, nobody's alone out there, a lot of people share the same emotions, feelings, experiences. Don't beat yourself up over it."

I took another sip of my drink, the smoky warmth of the bourbon etching a trail down my throat, sending a shot of fire back up once it hit the stomach. "You just captured it so perfectly, so succinctly," I said, "are you sure you're not a psychologist?"

She laughed. "Hardly, I've just been available to listen to a lot of my friends, and I've heard just about everything. And I've had my share of these sorts of things too."

Her hand was still on mine. I turned mine over and curled my fingers over hers, and she did the same. I looked up at her. "So, you really want to hear about my high school sweetheart?"

"Only if you want me to, or if you feel like talking about it."

So for the next 5 minutes I told her about Natalie, about our time spent in high school, about how we parted ways and didn't see each other again, and about how I stumbled upon her two nights ago. I told her that it wasn't so much of a great soul mate that was lost, but rather a love that ended unfinished, and that I felt not only a sense of loss over it, but now that Natalie was gone I felt a sense of having let her down so many years ago, and then never getting the chance to make things right.

Leannette sat and listened, and her hand gripped mine with more strength and support as the story progressed. When I told her about Natalie's death, and about my visit to her grave, Leannette leaned over and wrapped her arms around me in a comforting hug. When she let go, she said, "Why did you feel that you needed to make anything right? I mean, you didn't cheat on her, dump her for someone else, it sounds like it was typical high school first love and all, no harm no foul. What did you feel responsible for?"

I thought for a second, then said, "I felt like if I hadn't gone away to school, we could've stayed together, or maybe even going away we should have given it a chance, you know, see each other when I come back, . . ."

"Sure, sure, see her at holidays, long talks at night on the phone, and hundreds of miles away, really, . . .you know you did the right thing, the same thing that millions of kids have done, and do, at the end of every year. You needed to go out and become more of yourself, and she needed the same thing, and it's nobody's fault that you broke up, that's what high school kids do.

"And the other thing is, if it was so traumatic for her, why didn't she come looking for you, both after college, heck why didn't she try to keep it going with phone calls and letters when she was still a senior, . . . she let it go as much as you let it go, only it sounds like she really did let it go."

I looked at her and nodded. "Yeah, I know, I know all of this."

"And you know, then, that in all these years, she could've searched for you and found you, heck, you were still in the same area you grew up, for the most part, she could have come to you for closure, but she didn't. When you left she cried, which was her closure. You've been carrying this alone, because I'm not sure she was. You need to not own this like it's a scar. It's life, you need to let it go.

"Believe me, I've known you for, what, three, four hours? And I can tell, from how you've acted, from what you've said, from the stories you've told me, that you're a person who cares and loves deeply, and when you're in you're probably really all in, and that's great, that's what makes women love you, that your love and care and emotion is so genuine and real. But God, Wade, don't ever think that you need to 'love' the wrong out of relationships, or love someone to heal them, and that if you don't you're at fault." She turned toward me, close, with both hands holding mine. "Love yourself as much as you love others, as much as others love you. That's all you need to do."

I looked at her, her beautiful, knowing green eyes, the soft power and insight that lay deep behind them, and her warm, caring smile. She was looking at me, and at the same time we leaned toward each other and kissed.

Feeding the Wolf

Monday, October 20

I rolled over, letting go of the small pillow I had apparently been hugging for the last few hours. Picking up my head, I tried to place where I was; windows to the left, small sink to the right, and that thing in front of me, that might be . . . yeah, that looks like a TV. Ah, yes; I'm on the foldaway bed in the sitting room of my hotel room. And Leannette was sleeping in the bedroom.

I sat up, scratched my head, looked around. Looked down; yup, wearing shorts and t-shirt, my standard sleeping garb. I stood up and walked to the sink that was part of the tiny kitchenette and poured myself a glass of water. As I was drinking, the door to the bedroom opened, and Leannette stood there, wearing cute blue pajamas festooned with coffee cups. Coffee. Yeah, coffee would be really, really good right now.

God, she looked adorable, her hair tousled, sleep in her eyes, toenails that matched her Jamaican themed fingernails. Nobody – and I mean NOBODY! – should be allowed to look that cuddly and cute and warm and inviting after just rolling out of bed, especially not while wearing coffee cup jammies.

"You're up," I said.

"I've been up for a while, I was waiting until I heard you up before I came out, I didn't want to wake you."

"Love the coffee cups, they're cute."

She curtsied, then said, "I could use some of the real stuff."

"Me too," I said, "let me throw on jeans and a shirt and I'll run downstairs and grab some for us."

"Oh God, you're wonderful," she said, "if they have French Vanilla creamer, that's what I'd like. If not, the regular stuff will do."

"Will do." She retreated back into the bedroom. I quickly jumped into my jeans, threw a sweatshirt on over my t-shirt, slid my feet into my shoes, and hustled downstairs to the breakfast bar. Five minutes later I was back in the room with two large cups of coffee and three small French Vanilla creamer cups. I placed the cups on the table, and as I did I heard the shower running. Another five minutes and Leannette appeared from the bedroom, clean clothes and wet hair and still barefoot.

"Thank you," she said as she took the cup and started pouring some of the creamer in, "and thank God for coffee."

"You're welcome, and yes, thank God for coffee. They say they serve Starbucks, so it should be good, in theory at least."

"Mmmm, oh, it's perfect," she said after her first careful sip. "I'm done with the shower, so if you want you can take your turn, I'll sit out here and get lost in my coffee and check out what passes for morning TV in Albuquerque."

"Deal," I said, and I grabbed some clean clothes and disappeared into the bathroom. The water was as hot as the coffee, and I almost let myself linger, but I thought of her waiting and hurried to get dry and dressed and ready to go. I came out of the bathroom and found her sitting on the sofa, feet up on the table, nursing her coffee while intently watching a television anchor interview a woman holding a huge pepper. She motioned me over without looking away from the screen.

"You've gotta see this," she said, "this woman somewhere around here has a sixteen pound hot pepper, it's crazy."

I sat next to her, and together we sipped our coffee and watched in rapt silence as the woman on TV told all about her massive chile pepper, and displayed it proudly as if it were a small child in a pageant. It was surreal, and we couldn't stop watching. When the spot ended and the station went to commercial, we turned to each other.

"The things you see," I said.

"Big, crazy world," she replied. She smiled, then leaned over gave me a quick kiss on the cheek. "Good morning, you. You okay after last night?"

"Good morning to you, too," I said. "Sure, I'm fine, why? Was I drinking too much or something, I don't think I did, did it seem like, . . ."

"No, no, not that, just with all the soul spilling and talking and all the stuff with your high school, what was it, Natalie? All that stuff, I was just concerned you were going to have a hard time sleeping, that's all. Just want to make sure you're dealing with everything all right."

"I'm good, thank you," and I leaned over and kissed her cheek. "I appreciate your care and concern, but actually talking about it last night really helped me come to grips with it a bit more, I think everything being 'out loud' and on the table, you know, you talk about it and hear the words and it's more real, and I think that helped me accept what happened. So now it's just me moving along, and learning from it all, and keeping it all in mind so I live it, that's all, I need to not forget the good, and I need to not forget to take care of myself once in a while."

"That's good, 'cause you can't love anyone else til ya love yourself." She took another sip of coffee, then said, "So what's on the agenda for today? More driving?"

"Well, I should be able to make it to Sedona by mid-afternoon, so yeah, final leg of the drive. Which kinda brings up," I said, "what about you? What are your travel plans?"

"Okay, so let's talk about all of this," she said, and she placed her coffee on the table and turned to face me. "We met yesterday, we had dinner, we spent the night talking, we kissed more than once and neither of us has complained about it, so that's good, and I spent the night in your bedroom while you slept on the couch." She stopped, and looked at me for a moment. "So what's up with us? Is there an 'us'? Or was there just a night, two ships and all, and this is just nuts and we're pushing things and I really should go on to San Diego?"

I didn't reply immediately, but gave her a thoughtful look. After maybe 20 seconds of silence I said, "Is it too soon, or to presumptuous, for me to want there to be an 'us' even though we've known each other for less than 24 hours? Because I like you, I like being with you, and I'd love to get to know you better, but that kinda requires, . . ."

"Yeah," she said, "it requires us to be together, at least in the same general geographic area. And for the record, I feel the same way you do, something just clicked and I'm glad it did, I wasn't exactly looking for it or expecting it, but fate, or whatever, . . . we're here, and there's a reason, and it seems like we both want to see what more might be there."

"So that being said," and I took a deep breath, "come with me, at least until Flagstaff, and if you decide after 5 hours of being in a car with me that maybe this isn't the right thing, you can get a train or bus to the coast from there, but if it's all good and we want to continue, we can." We just looked at each other for a moment, then I said, "Whaddaya say, you up for the adventure?"

She tilted her head as she was so fond of doing, then a slow smile crept over her face and she said, "Like I said yesterday, my mom would shit bricks if she knew what I was doing, but yes, let's do this, let's go to Flagstaff and then see what fate wants us to do." She jumped toward me, wrapping her arms around me in a hug, and said "This may be crazy, but this feels right-crazy, if that makes sense. Crazy in a good, hopeful way."

I kissed her and said, "Sometimes crazy is good."

We jumped back from the hug and she said, "Give me 2 minutes and I'll be ready," then hurried into the bedroom to grab her things. I gathered my clothes, toothbrush, shampoo, and had my bag packed and zipped when she came out form the bedroom, full bag intact and bursting. "Okay, let's go."

I opened the door for her, and after we exited together I let it shut with a thunk. Day four of my trip was going to be interesting.

The first few hours of the drive that morning happened in cold and cloudy conditions, but we were so talkative that we hardly noticed. We talked about everything: jobs, friends, family, past loves, no subject was taboo or off-the-table. I learned that her parents were divorced, her mother still in St. Paul but her father now living on the gulf coast of Florida. She has a younger brother, Kyle, who was newly married to Lauren and living in Des Moines, near where he went to college at University of Iowa. Her last surviving grandparent, her maternal grandmother, was living back in Ireland, preferring to spend her last years in the land where she grew up.

I told her about my sister Beth, her husband Aaron, and their daughter Julia. I told her about my mom, and about the fire that occurred a couple days ago in my mother's condo complex. I told her about my friends in Chicago who threw me the going away party. I even told her about Elena, and the difficult to define relationship we had the past few years. And we talked more about Dave, and then about Sarah and her family, particularly her sister Anne. For two hours, very little silence in the car.

We made a quick stop for more coffee in Gallup, where Leannette picked up a box of powder sugared donuts, which we proceeded to attempt to eat while driving without getting covered in white powder. It was predictably unsuccessful, although it did allow us to laugh at ourselves and each other for the sheer breadth of places we were able to get sugar, not only on us but in the car. When we gave up with the donuts, she turned on the radio. "Ooh, look at you, mister fancy with XM radio. Let's see," she said, "what kind of music do you have preset here?" She punched each of the buttons, listening for a few seconds to what played, then continued on, not so much searching for the right song or style of songs but researching what I liked, what my musical tastes really were. She hit pay-dirt on the fifth button.

"Oh, Richard Thompson, I love Richard Thompson," she squealed, "I love this song."

"No kidding," I replied, "I like him too, not a lot of people are really aware of him but I think he's fantastic."

Instead of replying, Leannette started singing along with the song, bobbing and shaking her head, dancing in her seat. I laughed and started singing along, and soon we were shouting out with the song, insisting that "we'll never give it up."

"That song keeps me going," she said when it was over, "that song makes me feel like, life, whatever you throw at me, I'm gonna keep going, I'm never giving up."

"Sounds like the perfect song for your trip," I said, "or our trip. Or maybe just the perfect song for us right now."

"Oh neat, we have a song," she said, then kissed my cheek. "Oh, and look, we're in Arizona!" And there was the sign as we passed, welcoming us to Arizona. The final leg. Almost home.

We hadn't gone more than a mile when we came upon a roadside shop advertising authentic Navajo Jewelry and Pottery, and the shop itself was in the shape of a huge tepee. "Oh my God, Wade, would you look at that, we have to stop there," she said, so I pulled off at the exit and pulled into the parking lot.

When the car stopped she jumped out and hurried toward the storefront. "Okay, you gotta take a picture of me here," she said, and she tossed me her phone. I caught it but placed it in my pocket.

"How about I take one with my phone and text it to you?"

"Cool." A pause. "Do you have my number?"

I laughed. "Of all things, no, not yet. But I will in a moment." I held the camera phone to my eye, and she assumed a goofy pose in front of the huge yellow and red tepee with the sign on top. One click and she was immortalized forever. "Oh, perfect," I said, looking at it, "So where do I send it?"

"952-337-8469."

I punched the number into my phone, sent the picture via text, then went back and created a contact entry for her with that number. When I was done and looked up she was already entering the store. I ran to catch up, her phone in my pocket buzzing with the arrival of the text message I just sent.

I caught up to her inside, standing just past the door, looking around, taking it all in. It was nowhere near as expansive as Clines Corners yesterday, but it had a distinctly more authentic Native American feel, with western themed paintings, t-shirts, and sculptures, along with the requisite turquoise jewelry counter along the side of the store. We walked through the store, marveling at the variety of items, then paused at the jewelry counter, both of us looking in awe at the beautiful hand-made pieces on display. Bracelets, earrings, pendants, belt buckles – all of it stunning in its detail and beauty.

One piece jumped out at me, a woman's bracelet, brilliant tooled silver with 5 turquoise stone inlays formed to create what looked like a blue sunrise. It was simultaneously petite and heavy, appearing fragile while projecting strength and energy. I noticed Leannette was also looking at it. "That's gorgeous," I said, pointing at it.

"No doubt," she replied. "This stuff is so pretty."

"You should try that on," I said.

"Are you kidding, do you see the price, $355! No way."

A Navajo tradesman, perhaps the artist himself, was standing behind the counter. "Go ahead, please try it on," he said, "with your eyes and hair it will look beautiful on you." Without our asking he unlocked the case and brought out the bracelet, offering it for her to try on. She accepted it gingerly, and placed it on her right wrist.

"It's so smooth, and it's heavier than you would think from seeing it, but it's still so dainty," she, looking at it, turning her wrist over to see it from different angles. "It really is beautiful." One more glance, a heavy sigh, and she took it off and handed it back to the gentleman. Then she turned to me. "Beautiful, but too much for me to justify right now."

"When's your birthday?" I asked.

"Why?" When I didn't answer but simply smiled, she said, "No, no

116

way, you're not buying it for my birthday, which is in April by the way, no."

"Why not? Seems like I missed your last birthday."

"No."

"Oh, even better, Christmas is coming up, I can, . . ."

"No! Stop it, it's too much."

I took her hands in mine. "Listen, you and I both like it, right? And if it were maybe fifty bucks it wouldn't be an issue, right?"

"But it's not fifty bucks, it's over three hundred, . . ."

"Right, so it's more than you would normally spend on an impulse purchase. But two things here. First, we may never get up here again, to this little store on the westbound side of the highway." She looked at me with tilted-head skepticism. "And second, I think it's highly appropriate for one of us to have some sort of tangible memento or remembrance of us, this trip, what's happening and has happened yesterday and today, and I think this is perfect given where we met and where we're going."

"Jesus, Wade, . . ."

"Please? Let me buy this for you, no strings attached, just as a marker in time of us, and today." She didn't say anything. "Please," I asked again, and her face softened.

The man behind the counter, watching this play out, smiled and said, "I think I can take a little off this, how about $250? Would that make it more acceptable for the lady?"

"Leannette, see, only $250, this is meant to be," I replied to her.

"You're not going to let me leave here without it, are you?"

"It's one of my lovable traits you haven't learned yet."

"Okay, . . God, it's, . . . okay, fine. You can buy it with my limited blessing."

The man at the counter removed the tiny price sticker and handed the bracelet to her. She placed it on her wrist, standing for a moment and looking at it as the sunlight through the windows shone off it and made it glow. I paid, got my receipt, and we headed back to the car.

We climbed in and I started the engine, but before I pulled out I turned toward her. She was looking at me, a smile on her face, a tiny tear in her eyes. "You okay?" I asked.

"This is so beautiful," she said, "and thank you, you really did not have to do this, this is, . . ."

"This is as beautiful as you are," I finished for her, and I leaned to her and kissed her, a soft kiss that grew stronger with her emotion, our arms holding each other as if he finally found something worth holding and didn't want to let go. Which was probably the truth.

When the kiss ended, she wiped the tears from her eyes. "You gonna be okay?" I asked.

"Yes, you fool," she said, "I'm okay, I'm wonderful, I'm very happy, not because of the bracelet, although it is beautiful, but I'm very happy because of who you are, and I'm happy because I'm with you, and to me that's pretty great."

I smiled and gave her one more quick peck on the cheek. "And you're pretty great, and I'm happy here with you as well, . . . and let's get to Flagstaff for lunch, okay."

"Good idea. Let's blow this popsicle stand." With that I put the car in gear and we headed west toward the largest mountain in the state.

The drive to Flagstaff seemed to pass more quickly than the actual two-and-a-half hours it took. Once Leannette and I let the emotion of the "bracelet moment" fade, the drive again turned to talk, music, and singing along with the occasional song on the radio. My phone beeped for an incoming text near Winslow, a message from Dan simply asking:

How's it going? All okay? Just checking in.

I dictated to my response to Leannette as she typed my reply for me:

All good, outside of Flagstaff, will call tomorrow. Plenty to tell, trip has been interesting.

"Oh, so I'm interesting," she said, grinning as she prodded me.

"Well if I reply, 'I met someone great at a roadside shop and she's traveling with me now to Flagstaff,' I think the phone would ring pretty damn immediately and I'd end up talking to him, which I'd rather not do right now, I'd rather spend my time with you. He can hear all about you tomorrow, when I'm not in a moving vehicle."

"You'd better tell him I'm more than just interesting."

An hour later a similar text arrived from my sister, which Leannette kindly replied for me an almost identical response as I sent to Dan. "Nice that the people in your life are concerned, and checking in on you," she said. "I've been gone three days myself, and not a peep from my brother or mom."

"Well be fair, you started out with people," I said, "And I started out alone. Your family probably still thinks you're with them on your way to

San Diego, right?"

"Oh crap, yeah," she said, "I should probably call my mom when we stop for lunch and let her know what's going on, I'd hate for her to think I'm in California for a while when I'm really in Arizona. Can't be fooling my mom."

"Yeah, they're like that, they kind of appreciate knowing where their kids are, even when the kids are grown."

"And especially when they're hundreds of miles away," she added.

Soon the towering snowcapped tops of the San Francisco Peaks came into view, with the city of Flagstaff nestled at its southern base. We made it just after noon, and got off I-40 headed toward the downtown area where I thought we could find better lunch options than roadside fast food. Plus, with Flagstaff being only 30 miles from Sedona, it would provide the first chance to look around at this town that would soon be so close to home.

We caught up with the Historic Route 66, which was now disguised as Flagstaff's main street, passing the equally historic Train Station and just blocks from Northern Arizona University. We parked and walked a bit until we found a funky burger shop, almost hidden from view behind some trees and fountains in the park that it sat alongside. It was a small white clapboard building that used to be a house, and it had a small, rusted mailbox in front with the flap lying open. I hesitated for a moment, then kept walking, trying to think of when I had seen this before. We went inside, grabbed a table, ordered lunch, and relaxed a bit knowing the journey was almost over.

"So your mom," I said, "what exactly are you going to tell her?"

"Oh, I've been thinking about that," she replied, "and the best I can come up with is pretty much the truth, that my ride had a family emergency and had to drop me off in New Mexico, and while there I ended up meeting someone who offered to drive me at least to Arizona."

"Am I at least interesting," I asked playfully, knowing she'd remember my text to Dan about my 'interesting trip.'

"You're more than interesting," she said with a grin, "but for the first conversation, until my mom is certain that her little girl is safe and sound, you'll need to be honest and trustworthy."

"I can live with that. When are you gonna call her?"

"I'm thinking maybe after lunch. But hey, tell me about your place in Sedona. Where is it, by the way, and how did you get it? How do you even know what or where it is?"

"There's this thing called the Internet," I said, to which she threw her napkin at me.

"I get that," she said, "I mean how did you arrange for it, is it a rental, did you buy a place sight unseen, what's the deal?"

"Condo, west part of Sedona away from all the tourist stuff, rent-to-buy, so I looked at the pictures, guy sent me a video tour, I liked it enough to sign a six-month lease with option for more, and option to buy should I like it."

"Sounds nice," she replied.

"Hope so. And it has two bedrooms and a den, so no problem should you choose to come with me."

"Which I've been thinking about," she said, "especially since here we are in Flagstaff, where decisions need to be made."

"Yeah, I've been thinking about it as well."

"Well, here's what I think," she offered up. "It's just far too soon to be shacking up together."

"That does seem the sensible route."

"But here we are, and if not now, when? I mean, this sort of thing, this connection, doesn't happen. Okay, it happened for us, so maybe, if you're lucky, it happens once per life – IF you're lucky. And I think we're lucky. At least, I think I'm lucky.

"So despite it being illogical and insane and abrupt and sudden, I don't want to let us go. I want to see what happens to and with us, and I want to follow this feeling and this connection. And if that means zigging where I thought I'd be zagging, so be it.

"Having said all that, I do feel like I need time and space. I mean, I did decide to get away from a bad relationship too, and I was wanting to clear my life, and I was in no way thinking about any new relationships. I just want time for me to heal. So to me, that plays a part in how I feel, and any decisions I make as well."

"So," I said, "I get all of that, I get how you're feeling, and believe me, I feel a lot of that too. And I know it sounds, at least to me, like you're saying San Diego, and I think on a purely logical level that's the right decision, the 'no regrets' decision, and . . ."

"No, no," she piped in, "It's not about regrets or not, it's about not getting swept away in a moment that, while it feels wonderful, it's still a moment, and a new moment at that."

We were silent for a few moments, then I said, "So San Diego then."

She took a sip of her tea. "Why are there only two choices, San Diego or Sedona? Why can't there be a third or fourth choice, or hundreds of choices?" When I didn't say anything she continued. "I think I'm going to stay in Flagstaff for a few days, think about life, decide what I want and where I want to go and be, and then make the decision from there. No rushing things, no getting swept up in 'now' when I have a whole life ahead of me."

"But why stay here, paying to be here, when you could just come along with me, 30 miles away, and not have to, . . ."

"It's not about money Wade, and you know that, at least you should know that. It's about me making sure I'm being true to myself, just the same way me leaving Dave was, or the same way you leaving Sarah. It's a pause to make sure I'm true and fair to myself instead of rushing my life." She reached over the table and took my hands in hers. "And do not think for a second this means I'm saying goodbye to you, or giving up on what we seem to have here. That's one reason why I think Flagstaff is good, it's close to you but not too close, it'll allow us, if I stay here, . . ."

"If?"

"Gimme a chance, if I stay here, which who knows, I might chose to do that, it'll let us get to know each other and grow something, I don't know, more organically? More naturally? Just let it grow on its own, its own time."

She paused again, and we looked at each other. "But, if," I said, "If you stay. That's a big if."

"And moving down to Sedona with you is also a big if. Moving to San Diego alone is a big if. You moving to Sedona, 'if'." She sat back. "Everything we do, we do because we think it's the best decision, the best option at the time, and you and I make these decisions after thinking for a bit. How long did you say it took you to decide to leave Sarah, what was it, a few years?"

"Not the same," I said.

"A decision that affected your life for years to come, same sort of thing as both of us right now." She leaned over the table again and grabbed both of my hands. "I want both of us, you and me both, to do what's right for each of us, as individual people, before we do what's right for us as a couple. Please tell me, after all we talked about the past, about previous relationships, tell me that that's what you value as well."

I stared into her beautiful green eyes. "Damn it, do you have to be beautiful and right?" I leaned toward her and kissed her.

She smiled. "So I'm beautiful, huh?" But before either of us could answer, the server arrived with our burgers.

We both grabbed our food and dug in. After a satisfying first bite, I asked, "Okay, so you stay here in Flag for a bit, where? Find a hotel or something?"

She nodded, and said "For now, yeah, that would work just fine. Something close to town, I guess, since I have no car."

"A lot of walking. Hope the weather doesn't get bad too soon."

"Think warm," she said, and took another bite of her food.

The rest of lunch continued in that same vein, talking between mouthfuls of burgers and fries, deciding where she should stay, looking at the hotel apps on our phones for ideas and options. When we had both finished she decided on the Drury Inn, about four blocks from downtown along the main road that feeds to and from Route 17, Arizona's primary north-south highway. From there she could walk to downtown or the train station or bus depot, and it was rated high in safety, being situated next to NAU and probably hosting numerous parents during the course of the year. Once we were done and had paid the bill, we headed back to my car and made the quick drive to the hotel. I parked in front, and as we exited the car I said, "Why don't you go inside and see about a room, and I'll get your stuff together from the backseat and trunk and bring it all in for you."

"Thanks, that works, I'll meet you inside."

She walked to the entrance and the double doors automatically spread for her to enter through. I popped the trunk and grabbed her bag, and then made sure there was nothing else of hers left in the car. I grabbed a scarf that had fallen to the floor, and a travel mug that had held coffee but was now empty, closed the door, and made my way in.

She was finishing up at the front desk as I approached, and she turned just as I reached her. "All good?" I asked.

"For one week, yes," she replied. "Room 318."

"Okay then," I said, "Let's bring this stuff up."

"You don't have to, you know," she said. "You've been so good to me the past few days, you don't have to carry my things, escort me, all that, not if you want to get going and make it to your new place, I can manage just fine."

122

"No, this is no trouble, and heck, I'm already carrying this, it would be easier to just get in the elevator and go up than put it all down just for you to pick it all back up, no, let's go, I've got it."

"Well okay then, thank you." She turned and led us past the rack overflowing with travel and visitors brochures to the elevator. She pushed the button, and the doors opened immediately.

"You're magic," I said.

She smiled. "You didn't already figure that out?" She stepped into the elevator and I followed.

The doors opened to the third floor hallway in seconds. The sign on the wall pointed us left to get to her room, which was halfway down the hall. She slid the key card into the lock, and when the light turned green she twisted the handle and opened the door. We walked in; she went to open the curtains while I placed her items on the bed. When the room awakened to the flood of light, she turned and stepped back toward where I was standing.

"So," I said.

"So," she replied, "I think I'm good here."

"You sure?"

"Yeah, pretty sure." She smiled. "New adventure, right?"

We stood in our first uncomfortable silence for about ten seconds, then we both reached out to each other, wrapping our arms around the other in a hug. A few more seconds and we pulled away, pausing for a deep, warm kiss.

"Is it too early to miss you?" I asked.

"Nope. But hey, it's not goodbye, it's just, . . . I'm not sure exactly what it is, but is isn't goodbye. It's just see you later."

"Well, in that case, I'd better leave so later can get here sometime soon."

"Go," she said, pushing me away, "go find your new home, go find yourself, we'll talk soon, and later will get here when later is meant to get here."

"Okay." I leaned and gave her a last, quick kiss. "Let me know if you need anything, or if you don't, or just . . . just let me know."

"Of course. Now go."

I turned and walked to the door, opening it and looking back at her. She was still smiling, holding her scarf that she had picked up from the bed, and she shook the fringed end at me. I smiled back and walked out, closing the door behind me.

I began my drive to Sedona feeling lonely. I didn't turn the radio on, preferring the quiet of the car and the road. I found route 89A, the scenic drive from Flagstaff to Sedona, and started the winding drive down through the cliffs and rocks and valleys that were carved into the landscape. It was a gorgeous drive, but I was distracted. Leannette, my mom, Natalie, Sarah, Elena – all of my relationships, past, present, perhaps future, weighed on my mind. I kept playing key parts over and over, trying to determine what I did that was wrong, was right, was plain infuriating. I played events from my life over in my mind but gave them different endings, took different paths to get to where I thought they should've ended up, but none of it made sense, and I kept returning to feeling that I had let so many people down.

About 25 minutes into the drive my phone rang. I looked down: my mom. I clicked the speaker, and before she could say anything said, "Hey mom, I'm driving, give me a second to pull over so I don't kill myself, just hold on." I pulled off onto a gravel drive, put the car into park, and picked up the phone. Switching speaker off, I said, "Okay mom, I stopped. Hey, what's up?"

"Hi honey, are you busy?"

"Just driving through some mountains, getting closer to Sedona. How are you?"

"Oh, not very good."

"Why? What's going on? You okay?"

"I talked to Evelyn, my neighbor from down the hall, and she was saying the fire really damaged the building worse than we thought."

Not good. "Geez mom, how bad is it?"

"Well, Evelyn said the investigator called it a firetrap, that there weren't enough alarms and sprinklers, and that for a building of that size it should have had more safety features, but it didn't and that's why the fire caught so quickly and spread." When I didn't say anything for a second, she continued. "I still don't know when they'll let us go back and get more of our belongings, and now I'm worried that we'll never get in, that they'll need to knock it down."

"Oh mom, they won't do that, not with everybody's lives still in there, they'll let you back soon, I'm sure."

She was quiet for a moment, then said, "So you don't think you can

124

come home at this point?"

"Why mom, I can't re-build the condo, and I have no house there, so I'd have nowhere to stay, and there's really nothing I can do."

"But it would be nice to have you here, that's all. It would make me feel better."

"I thought Julia was trying to make you feel better, playing nurse to Grandma."

"It's not the same," she said with a weary voice. "It would just be good to have both kids here for me right now."

"Well mom," I said with a sigh, "you'll have to settle for one kid there and the other available by phone. Maybe, once I get settled, I can fly back for a weekend, maybe that would work."

"It wouldn't be the same," she said, "but if that's all you can do."

"Mom," I said, my voice raising in volume, "there's nothing I can do. I can, I will talk to you every day and check in to see how you are, but you're in good hands with Beth and Aaron and Julia and that'll have to do right now while I get my own life settled. Okay?"

"Are you in Arizona yet?"

"Yes, about 20 minutes from my new home, I'm on the road now."

"Well I should let you go then, and not take you away from your driving." Already forgot that I said I pulled over and stopped to talk. "You call when you can."

"I'll call you tomorrow."

"Oh, if you have time, that would be good, I'll be here."

"Okay mom, you get rest, okay? Love ya."

"Love you too, Wade." And I hung up.

And then I sat for a moment and swore at the steering wheel for a solid minute. So close – so damn close – to my new home, and now I'm feeling the pull to turn around and head home, turn around and take care of my surviving parent. It's what people do, they take care of their parents. They owe them that, especially since the parents spent so much time and money taking care of the kids for years.

Damn it.

For the next 10 minutes I sat in silence, car motor humming, the only sounds those of passing vehicles on the road. There were no easy answers to this. I wanted to begin my life, the next chapter of my life. But . . . heck, even Leannette mentioned how her ride down here turned around and headed home when it came to family emergencies, and she mentioned how normal that was to do. And really, what would it mean to drive back, spend a couple of days, maybe a week there, and then head back here again.

Damn it. That's so, so impractical. I'm here already – well, damn close, anyway. And it's not like she's there alone. She has my sister and her family. She's not alone. She doesn't need me.

But what if she does . . .

What if this sends her downhill, she gets ill, . . .

God damn it.

I looked out the windshield at the trees as they swayed in rhythm with the breeze, and saw the colors of the rocks peeking between the branches. A lone hawk spiraled overhead, probably wondering what this strange metal object was, and why it was spoiling the setting. I followed its flight, then was distracted by a smaller bird, fighting mightily against the breeze to reach a tree. I watched as it landed on a small birdhouse. He went in, then came right back out and again took flight. He couldn't make up his mind either.

Well, okay, I was this close, I might as well find my condo, get the keys, and decide from there what my next step would be. I put the car into gear, circled around, and pulled out onto the road. I was completed unprepared for the sight of a pickup truck barreling down the road, coming toward me in my lane.

I flashed my lights, but he didn't sway. I took my foot off the gas, and steered toward the right shoulder. Well, where the right shoulder usually is. On this stretch of 89A, there was only maybe half a foot of gravel, followed by a gradual decline toward a stream. I looked back at the road, at the truck coming closer, now weaving between both lanes. Until he was maybe 50 yards from me, and heading straight toward me.

I hit the horn, stomped both feet on my brakes, and turned as hard as I could toward the right shoulder. The truck whistled past me, barely missing my front fender, never slowing. My car skidded off the road, missing any trees or shrubs, then began a jarring sideways slide down the embankment. I bumped the door, bounced against the steering wheel, and was generally abused as the car ambled over the shrubbery and finally came to rest just short of the water. As the car stopped I heard another horn, then the sickening crunch of metal being compacted and twisted intermingled with shattering glass.

I sat stunned for a few moments, trying to take in what had happened, and then trying to move my various body parts that had been treated so rudely by the descent. When I was satisfied that there was no blood nor broken bones I pushed the door open and climbed out of the car. I walked around the vehicle, assessing the damage, of which, thankfully, there was little beyond scrapes to the fenders and colored smears on the doors where the car's body slid through the foliage. Knowing that what occurred on the road must've been much worse that what happened to me, I climbed up the embankment, twisting my knee as I scrambled to the road. Once there, I saw the mangled wreckage of the pickup truck, upside down on the pavement, while another vehicle, what had been a Toyota moments ago, was sitting shredded, parts and scraps scattered along the road, the car itself compressed to 65% of its original size.

Hearing no sirens, I made my way back down to my car, found my phone where it had been thrown under my seat, and dialed 911. After giving account of where we were and what had happened, I made my way again up the ridge, thinking I should help but not sure if there was anyone left living to offer assistance to. By the time I made the road two other cars had stopped, and the occupants of those vehicles were milling about wreckage, trying to see if there was anyone needing help. One person saw me and shouted, "Hey, there's another one over here," and started running toward me. I met him on the road, told him what had happened and where my car was, and together we went to help the others, hoping there was life somewhere in the mess.

Moments later we could hear the faint whine of sirens, and they came closer and louder until we saw the dance of red and white lights bounce off the trees and announce the arrival of the emergency crews. Two police cars and an EMT unit stopped yards from the closest car, and the officers jumped out to assess the scene. I stood watching, all of the activity seeming to happen slowly. People were running and calling and whistling, and I know they were doing so in great urgency, but to me it all seemed to be happening in slow motion. I turned; someone was pointing at me, and as if by magic a police officer was next to me, talking to me, asking me what happened. I explained what I had seen – the pickup truck speeding toward me in the wrong lane, my driving off the road to avoid a certain collision, and then the sounds of the wreck. An EMT was then leading me toward the open rear door of a medical vehicle. She sat me down, took my pulse, and did various checks that I was in no mood to disagree with. She pronounced me alive, but made me sit there, and told me to sip the red liquid from the bottle that appeared from nowhere.

For the next three hours I sat either in the rear of the EMT unit or in the backseat of one of the police cars, telling my story numerous times. Each time the officer nodded, and they eventually let me know that my story seemed legit based on skid marks, physical evidence, and witness statements. Two people had died; another two were airlifted to Flagstaff, the nearest trauma center. Route 89A was closed for over 2 hours. A tow truck came and fished my car out of the gully.

I had ample time to think, even if my mind was not in prime shape. Seeing the paramedics wheel the bagged bodies away was more than sobering; that could've been me. It made me consider all that had been on my mind prior to the accident. It made me re-think that conversation with my mother. It caused me to cry, to get angry, to pray to a God I wasn't sure was out there. It also led me to the realization that if something had happened to me, I'd never see my family again. Never see my mom. My sister. My niece. All the people I loved.

Just before 5:30 the scene was finally cleared. I had tested my car, and found it started and ran properly. There was surface damage, and the front end would need an alignment sooner rather than later, but otherwise it was drivable. Tires fine, lights fine, brakes fine. I was released to go. I sent a quick text on my phone and, sure it was delivered, fired the engine and pulled out very carefully onto the road. Heading north.

My car died just as I was entering Flagstaff. It lurched, coughed, and then gave up. It did all this slowly enough for me to move out of the I-17 traffic and onto the right shoulder. I dialed AAA, only to discover that my membership in the Illinois AAA didn't automatically transfer to the AAA in Arizona. I must've sounded about as flustered and sorry as I felt, because the local AAA rep agreed to waive the costs and send someone out to help. I guess in some ways it does pay to have a shitty afternoon.

I sat off the side of the road, the late afternoon sunset casting a final glow over the pines that ringed the San Francisco Peaks. It was starting to get chilly, and I hoped that the wait for AAA wouldn't be too long. While I counted the cars to pass time I thought about the trip so far, as it stood. Three days, within 40 miles of my destination – and I felt as lost and confused and far away from Sedona as I did a year ago. Maybe Elena and my mom were right, maybe beautiful scenery is simply that, something to look at while life continues, something that allows you to stop focusing on what really matters. Yes, the mountains are beautiful. No, looking at them for five minutes doesn't change anything in life.

A moment later the AAA truck pulled up and stopped just behind my sad Solara. The driver took a look at the car as he walked toward me. "Uhm, wow, it looks like you were in an accident or something." After I explained my afternoon on 89A, he nodded and popped the hood. "Oh, yeah, sure, here ya go," he said, "your fuel pump's busted." I leaned over the fender to look, and he pointed at the pump, where I could see the fuel line dangling where it should've been connected to the pump.

"Crap. How bad?" I asked.

"Nothing I can fix here," he replied. "I'll tow ya to our garage in Flag, they can tell ya more about it once they look at it."

Great, just great.

Twenty minutes later the AAA truck deposited me and my car at a small repair shop on the eastern edge of downtown Flagstaff. The manager said it would probably be at least two days for them to get parts and then fix the car, but they would have a car to rent me – tomorrow. Where was I staying, and when could I come back to pick it up? I thanked him, told him I'd call tomorrow about the rental, grabbed my bag from the passenger side floor, and headed back toward the center of town on foot.

By 7:15 the sun had set, and I found myself at the bar of a simple, rustic restaurant in downtown Flagstaff. The beer choices were basic, the food choices even more so, but I really didn't care. I sat nursing a beer and a burger, alternately thinking I should call Leannette, and thinking that it seemed too needy to be calling her later the same day we decided to give ourselves some time to think. Truth be told, I was secretly wishing and hoping she'd suddenly walk in and sit down next to me, and I would tell her all about this day and get a warm hug in return. By 8:30 I told myself that she wasn't magically appearing, and I should get on with what I needed to do. Which meant paying the tab and making the short walk to the train station.

Flagstaff's train station was a historic brick building smack dab in the middle of town. The Amtrak trains stopped there twice a day, once heading west to Los Angeles, and once heading east to Chicago. I had no idea what time the trains made their stops, or what the cost of a ticket was, but I thought, given everything the day had communicated to me, that I should at least price a ticket and see what options were available for me.

A single light above the door was on, casting a halo around the decades old "Flagstaff" sign that hung heavy on the wall. I pulled the door open and entered a simple room, ticket booth on the right, waiting area with carved wooden benches to the left. A faded yellow shade was pulled down at the ticket window, and as I stepped toward it I could see the small sign hanging from the window: "Closed. Reopen at 9:00PM." I looked up at the clock on the wall; 8:40. That wasn't so bad, a twenty minute wait. I turned and walked to the waiting area, where no one was waiting, and sat down on the bench that afforded the best view of the window.

Moments after I sat, the door opened, and an older Native American gentleman walked in. His dusty western hat was perched askew on his head, his jet-black pony-tail flowing down his back over his heavy coat. He wore worn suede boots, and carried nothing but a small fanny pack. He had the weathered, leathery look of a tribal elder who had lived a lifetime out in the sun and wind. He took a quick look around the room then sat on the bench across from me. Once seated he smiled at me and nodded. I nodded back.

"Ticket booth opens in about twenty minutes," I said.

"Where are you headed?" he asked.

I let out a deep breath and shook my head. "Well, . . ." I paused, "possibly Chicago. Possibly nowhere."

He smiled. "You don't have to wait here for twenty minutes to go nowhere, unless this waiting room is the nowhere you're seeking."

"It's, it's complicated," I said. "I'm trying to decide if I stay here or head back home, back to Chicago, where I'm from. This day, . . ." and I paused again, looked around the room.

"Bad day?" he asked.

"Started good, turned bad, leaving me unsure of what to do or which direction to go."

He nodded. "What was your destination this morning, when the day started good, as you say?"

"Sedona," I replied, "I was headed toward Sedona, toward what I thought would be my new home."

"Ah, new life, new course, new place to call home."

130

"Right," I said. "But enough has happened today that, well, . . . I wonder if making a new home there now is the right thing to do."

"So when you woke up, Sedona was the future. What happened today that makes you think going backward toward the past is better than going forward toward the future? Or that you'll find what you're looking for by retracing your steps?"

I wasn't sure how to respond. My whole trip up until now had been me trying to "find" a new life, a new path, a new sense of where I belong. The accident, the call (among many) from my mom, my nagging sense of disappointing my family and friends – it all had made me wonder if I was selfish for distancing myself from the people and places I loved. Moving to Sedona, that didn't guarantee I'd find anything. Well sure, the trip did allow me to meet Leannette, but was that a blip, or something more? All my decision to move to Sedona did was ensure that from this day forward my environment would be new, allowing me to explore new things, new places, new people. Create new memories. Adjust my days and nights and work and play in different directions. If I chose.

"Well," I said, "I'm . . . I'm just wondering at this point if I made the right decision, and if this really is the right thing for me to be doing right now, at this point in my life."

"You've made it quite far for having doubts."

I smiled. "I had fewer doubts yesterday. But today, . . ."

He nodded. "Today things changed."

"Right. Today, I don't know . . . it seems like something, karma, God, whatever, was trying to tell me something, trying to get me to rethink being here. And then my mother back home, she's having a tough time, . . ."

"No mother is ever happy seeing her son leave the nest," he said. "Even the strongest women shed a tear when the son leaves home. Can I ask, are you the eldest son?"

I nodded. "Yes."

He nodded back. "Yes, very difficult for her. She is now alone, then?"

"No, my sister is with her, my sister and her family. My father is gone." I was quiet for a moment. "She really didn't want me, or doesn't want me, to move all the way out here. She's afraid she'll never see me again."

"Fear is a strong emotion. And one that's easily triggered, easily accepted, and easily shared."

I let out a heavy breath. "So that leaves me here, sitting in the station, not sure of what I'm doing, where I'm going, . . ."

"Remaining here will cause you to feel guilt, as if you are turning your back on your mother." he said. I nodded. "And returning home will cause you to feel resentment, as if you are turning your back on yourself." Another nod from me. "You are taking on the feelings and emotions of others," he said. "What about the feelings you own? Where is your love, your joy?"

"I really don't know," I said. "And that's what has me so confused. I may have found something worth being out here for, but it's too early to tell, and it may be nothing. At the same time, there are plenty of people back home who I love and am close to, so . . . that complicates the decision. I could be happy or unhappy in either place. There is no right place, I suppose."

The old man slowly stood, then stepped over to my bench and sat down next to me. "There is a right place. But only you can find it. It's your right place, nobody else's."

"I don't know," I replied. "I mean, that sounds great, it sounds wonderfully spiritual and all, but in real life it seems like there can be more than one right place to be, and it seems like the tough thing is finding which place to be and when."

The old man sat silent for a moment, then turned to look at me. He placed a hand on my shoulder, then said, "What is it that you want? What is it that will make you happy?"

"I guess, the same as everyone . . . love, family, doing something rewarding, . . ."

He waved a hand at me. "No, if it was that simple, why leave your home in Chicago?" When I didn't reply he continued. "What is it that sent you on this quest, was is it about starting new in a new place that you want, that you think will bring you happiness? And more happiness than if you had stayed home?"

I thought for a few moments. What was I trying to find? "Well," I said, "Sometimes I think I want to kinda start over again. I've made so many bad decisions, I've wasted so much time in my life, I just . . . I just want to feel like I have a clean slate, and can try to build what I think is the best me possible." I looked up at him. "Is that too much to ask?" When he didn't reply, I continued. "And can I ask, why are you so interested in me, and why I'm here?"

"You looked lost," he replied.

132

"Well, tonight I feel lost," I said. "What would you do? Head home, or keep heading away from home?"

He smiled. "There's a Navajo saying that there are two wolves living inside each of us. One wolf is evil, filled with anger, guilt, resentment. The other wolf is good, filled with peace and love and hope. The wolf that wins out," and he leaned toward me and touched my chest with a finger, "is the one that you feed."

He sat back and looked at me. "Feed the right wolf."

Before I could say anything the door to the station opened, and a man and woman entered pushing their baby in a stroller. They made their way across the waiting room and unloaded their bags and baby onto an empty bench. Before they could even get situated the door creaked again, and another couple entered. I looked back at the clock: five minutes til 9:00. The ticket booth would be opening soon.

I turned toward the old man just as he rose from the bench. He looked toward me, smiled, nodded, then turned to walk out.

"Hey, wait a sec," I said, grabbing my bag and getting up to follow him. "Wait, wait, . . ." I walked quickly to catch up with him, which I did just outside the station. "Wait, what do you mean, feed the wolf?"

"Who are you living for?" he said as we walked.

"Who am I living for? Well, me, of course."

"Hmmmm," he grunted. We kept walking, his pace quick and steady for a man of his years. When he suddenly stopped, I almost walked past him, but caught myself and turned to face him.

"What now?" I asked.

"You have time?"

"For what?

"For discovering. For what comes next."

"I . . . sure, I suppose. What do you mean?"

He began walking again. "Come with me, I have something to show you, something I think will help you find your way. And your wolf."

I stood there as he stepped away ahead of me. When he was maybe 15 yards away he paused and turned, then motioned for me to join him. "Come, this way." He turned and kept walking. I ran to catch up.

We walked a block east of the train station, then turned south, crossing the rail tracks. A few blocks further, then another turn, again to the east. We were now in a neighborhood of small, older houses, including some branded as fraternities for Northern Arizona University, only a few blocks away. Many of the houses were ringed by rusted chain-link fences, while others were hidden behind funky painted wooden fences or trees and bushes that acted like sentry. At the end of this block we reached perhaps the smallest house on the street, a shabby structure encircled by a petite white picket fence. It was at this house that the old man turned, unlatched the gate, and walked to the door. I followed, closing the gate with a clack.

He unlocked the wooden front door and motioned for me to come in. Once inside, he reached back and flipped a switch, a small lamp coming to life and casting a bronze glow across one side of the small front room. I looked around: the walls were covered with paintings, while to the left there sat an easel and a table, multiple canvases leaning against the walls just behind the half-completed work perched on the easel.

"My studio," the old man said as he crossed the room and took off his coat. As he was moving and speaking I made my way to one of the paintings, and began carefully examining the artwork that blanketed the walls. They were heavy in Native American imagery (or so I thought), and were vividly drawn with dramatic blues and violets and yellows. I could see, at various times and in various pieces, coyotes, bears, eagles, people, huts, angel wings, even rows of corn. And as I moved, or as light glanced off the canvases in different angles, what I saw would change; what was a wolf was now a fish, or the mountain suddenly became a man sitting in prayer. On the lower right corner of each painting I saw, written in precise hand, the name of the artist: Carl Whitedog.

"Carl Whitedog . . . is that you?" I asked.

"Yes," he said, approaching me. "And you are?"

"Wade."

"Nice to meet you, Wade. There's something I want to show you, this one," he started to cross the room, "over here." He stopped in front of a large painting, one that almost covered the entire side wall. "Take your coat off, put your bag down. Come take a look."

I shook loose of my coat and placed it on a chair, my bag on top. Then I walked over to where he was standing and looked up at the picture. It was massive in scale and in scope, and I was overwhelmed by not only the detail but by the various points that seemed to be vying for my attention. There was so much to see, so much to take in. Where to start?

"This . . . . wow, this is gorgeous," I said. "So much to it, so much detail. So much that, even when you look at it, you're not sure you're seeing it all."

"It is called 'Nihalgai-Nakletso', The Wolf of the White World," he said. He then leaned forward and clicked on a dial, a small light fading up to illuminate the painting. "As you can see, much like life itself, different things become visible and easily seen when the light changes." He slowly turned the dial, and as the light decreased, then increased again, different elements appeared. What was an eagle became a cloud; the small huts, surrounded by people, became wolves howling at the moon. It was like that everywhere I looked.

"This is amazing," I said. "What does it all mean?"

"It is part of the story of our people, the Navajo, where we came from, and how we got to where we are today." He turned the dial and the light dimmed. "This, this mountain here," and he pointed, "This represents the white, or glittering world, the final world of four of which we sought. And the water that runs down the mountain," again he pointed, "represents the waters from the previous worlds that tried to catch those that escaped to this white world.

"Here are animals, a coyote, a water buffalo, and over here, blue flowers and corn are growing – all part of the life of the new world. And this child down here, in the corner, this is Turquoise Boy. He gave a sacred offering to the coyote, who promised in return a male child – Black Cloud. This child would bring thunder and lightning. And there would also be a female child – Female Rain. She, of course brought us the rain."

He turned the dial just a bit, and the increased light created subtle changes in what I was seeing. "But the water buffalo disappeared, taking all the water with her. That is why, now, the water, which was plain earlier, now you can barely see it. Now you see here, in the side of the mountain," he pointed, "can you see the family? This is the ancestral family, who built the mountains and created fire." Again, he turned the dial, allowing more and different detail to be seen. "And as the light is brighter you see how the fire is bringing light to the land." And I could see what were just a moment ago wisps of clouds were now obviously licks of fire.

"Now," he said," focus on the mountain." As I stared at the mountain the light slowly grew brighter, until the shadows and form of the mountain began to reveal itself as a wolf.

"Oh my god," I said, "the mountain is really a wolf." I looked at him. "That's amazing."

"The wolf, or coyote, is not only the symbol of health, but of the ability to find what is lost." He turned toward me. "You look deeper, let me get us some water." With that he walked to the kitchen.

I stared at the painting, trying to see what other mysteries were hidden within the frame. What I discovered was that I didn't need to really concentrate on an area, or try to determine hidden figures. It wasn't 'Where's Waldo.' The more I relaxed and just looked at the painting, the more the obvious appeared, and the more I could see figures and items simply as they were, within the larger context of what I thought I saw. It was all hidden in plain sight, easy for anyone to see as long as they were open to seeing it and not stressing over finding it.

He returned with two glasses of water, and handed one to me. "Thank you," I said as I accepted the glass. "This painting, what you've done here is amazing. I . . . every time I look at it I see something new, it's like the painting keeps unfolding right in front of me."

"There are many truths in the world, and many of them are not apparent until you are ready to see them. It is the same way with our beliefs and our traditions, they surround us, but we do not see until we're ready to see, and when we do open our eyes to them they become clear, and we then see them in everything. This is why I paint in this way, because life has so many things gently hidden, but when the eyes change, when the light changes, when our perspective changes – that's when we see all there is to see."

"Where did you learn this, learn to paint like this?"

"When I was young, I was always drawing. It came natural to me. Then, as I grew up, I grew more interested in the stories of the Navajo, and my people and my heritage. I wanted to find a way to put the Navajo stories and the stories of people – my people, all people – onto canvas, a way to show life, and let people see and experience the stories." He motioned toward the artwork that filled the room. "And this is what I've done, all this. The stories of my ancestors. The stories of the Navajo." He turned toward me. "The stories of people."

We stood in silence for a moment, then I turned to him. "Why did you speak to me at the station tonight? And why did you bring me here?" When he didn't answer, I said, "There must've been something, some reason, for you to come into the train station and, and find me, and talk to me. And then some reason for you to want me to see this painting."

"I noticed you walking down Santa Fe, toward the station," he said, "and I could see in your walk that you were upset, that you were searching for a direction, searching for answers. Your manner, the way you held yourself, as if you were a spectator in your own body . . . you did not have a purposeful stride." He stopped and took a sip of water. "You seemed to be without vision. You seemed lost."

"And you rescue the lost, like puppies?"

"I cannot rescue anyone," he said. "We can only rescue ourselves. But sometimes I come across people who seem intent on rescuing themselves, but they seem to not know which way to look. For those people, I can sometimes help them find a direction, so that they may in turn find themselves."

"And from seeing me walking, you could tell I needed rescuing?"

"No, from watching you walk I could see you were searching. From talking to you, that's when I knew what you were searching for, and that you were on a quest of sorts, and that you needed to find your direction."

I wasn't sure how to respond, so I scanned the room and, seeing a small couch along the far wall, walked over to it and sat down. What. A. Day.

"Okay, well," I started, "Thank you, for speaking to me, for this, the paintings, . . . but I'm still not sure if forging ahead is the right move, or going back home to take care of my mom and continue the life I had is the right move. I'm still . . . I don't know, torn? Conflicted?"

"If it were a friend or family telling you this, what would you tell them?"

"I'd tell them to follow their heart. I mean, . . . seriously, I'd tell them to move forward, explore life, start over."

"Then you should tell yourself that as well. Be your own best friend."

"That's easier said than done," I replied. "I still gotta live with how I feel after I make my decision, I'll still be dealing with those pangs of, 'should I have done this or not, maybe I should've done that,' buyer's remorse sort of thing."

The old man said nothing, but then turned and walked back into the kitchen. I sat on the sofa, wondering if perhaps he'd be able to bring back a drink somewhat stronger than water. When he returned he was carrying nothing, not even his own water glass. As he passed the chair on which my coat and bag sat, he slightly brushed against it. As he did, an envelope fell to the floor. He stopped, looked at it, looked at me, then picked it up.

"I'm sorry, is this yours?" He walked over to me, then held it for me to take. I took it from his outstretched hand, then turned it over.

"Holy shit, I forgot all about this." My name on the front, in Natalie's handwriting. Her letter to me.

"Important?"

"Not sure," I said, "A couple of nights ago I happened upon the cousin of my high school girlfriend, my first love, and found out she passed away."

"Oh, I'm sorry, she must've been young."

"Yeah, well, I guess before she died she wrote some letters to people who'd been important in her life." I held up the envelope. "This is her letter to me."

"I see," he said. "So it is important."

"Don't know. Haven't read it yet."

"Why not?"

"Because, . . . well, I don't know, maybe I'm a little scared of what she wrote." I looked up at him. "I broke up with her when I left for college, and she took it pretty hard. I'm not sure I want her final words to me to be angry, I felt bad enough as it was back then."

"If she took the time to write it, you should most certainly take the time to read it." He sat down next to me. "You owe her that much."

"I was waiting for the right time."

"The right time is always now. There is no other time."

"All right," I said, "let's see what she said." I pulled on the corner of the envelope and carefully peeled the flap back, then reached in and pulled out the folded pieces of paper. I dropped the envelope on my lap, unfolded the pages, faced them right-side up, and began to read.

Dear Wade,

It's been quite a long time, hasn't it? I truly hope and wish you are doing well, and are happy and healthy in where your life has taken you. Me — well, if you're reading this, you know . . .

Over the past few weeks as I've been dealing with my "news," I've taken the time to think about my life and the people who have meant the most to me at the most important times of my life. And every time I think of high school, I think of you. Of us. Of that one fantastic, wondrous, magical year when we were inseparable and really grew up together.

I've wondered over the years how you are, if you followed your dreams, if you did those things we always talked about that would make you happy and feel like the person you were meant to be. Oh, I hope so! I hope you found truckloads of happiness, more than can fill a lifetime. You deserve it! So, are you a writer, like you always said you'd become? Have you written your first novel yet? Your first screenplay?

When we split up, it was so difficult for me, and for you too, I'm sure. At the time it felt like a great betrayal, like we were so meant be to together forever and we chose to throw it all away. Funny how, when you're 17, every crisis is "super-sized" and every emotion is ten times more dramatic than it really is. It took me a while to learn that, and to come to terms with it. I thought life would end when we broke up, but it was only a chapter that ended.

I learned so much from you – from us being "us." I learned to love myself for who I am. I learned to give myself over to someone else. I learned that being vulnerable is frightening and liberating, provided you're being vulnerable with (and to) someone who's also feeling vulnerable. And maybe most important, I learned to forgive – myself and others. When we broke up, I really hated you for being a year older, for leaving for college, for a year that seemed to go nowhere. And I hated myself for allowing me to be seduced by the "older guy," and hated myself for letting me fall so hard for you. I vowed to never do that again unless it was the real thing, and would be forever. But I learned love doesn't work that way, and that I can't prevent myself from feeling, from loving. So I had to forgive myself, so I could move forward and love someone else. And then I had to forgive you, because you didn't "do" anything to me except love me for who I was and then know when our time was up.

So, in this letter Wade, I'm telling you that I forgive you, and I forgive myself. And I really hope and pray that you haven't been carrying any anger or resentment with you for all these years, that you've not only moved on and grown but also forgiven me, and most importantly, forgiven yourself for anything you might have felt guilty for. Remember what I used to say to you? "Believe in yourself *as I believe in you." To that I add, "Forgive yourself and those who love you, as they have already done the same for you."*

Please always remember us, and remember the smiles, the laughter, and the love. And remember that who we are ended up being started with that year, and with us discovering how to love ourselves and each other. Remember me not with tears, but with hope — hope for yourself.

Laugh for me. Laugh a lot, for both of us.

With much love, Natalie

I would like to say that I followed her directive and laughed. I really would like to say that. But the truth is that halfway through her letter my eyes started getting wet, and by the time I finished reading all I could do was close my eyes and cry.

"Are you okay?" the old man said.

"I'm not sure."

"What did she tell you?"

I looked up. "She said she hopes I have a wonderful life . . . that she forgave me years an' years ago . . . and that I should forgive myself as well."

He smiled. "Which wolf are you going to feed?"

Tuesday, October 21

I rolled over and discovered I couldn't feel my right hand. I started shaking it, hoping it would spring to life, and after perhaps 30 seconds the numb turned to tingle, which turned to feeling. As I did this I looked around at the room, the old man's living room. Sleeping on the couch was a thoroughly college thing to do, but by the time the night had wound down and the talking and crying had ended I agreed to accept his offer to stay the night. Well, and besides: I really had nowhere else to go. I sat up, a pillow falling off me to the floor. Sunshine was seeping into the room, brushing his paintings with soft morning light, allowing them to appear newly hopeful and optimistic. What had seemed so serious in the sharp light of the lamp last night now looked inviting and soothing, as if his Navajo scenes were welcoming peace rather than illustrating the conflicts of life.

I stood and stretched, then took a few quiet steps through the home in search of my host. Finding no one else there, I poured myself a glass of water and returned to the living room. I picked up Natalie's letter and folded it back into the envelope, then placed it carefully into my duffel bag. A quick trip to the bathroom to wash my face, brush my teeth, put on a clean shirt, and fix my hair, and I was set. I hated dashing out without saying anything or thanking him for his kindness, but since he wasn't here . . .

I was twisting into my jacket, wondering exactly what my next move would be, when, as I neared the door, I saw another envelope, this one taped to the door, my name written on the front. I stopped, removed it, and opened it.

Wade,

* * *

Thank you for being my guest, and for allowing me to participate in your journey. You know what you need to do — you've always known it, I believe. It's now your time to believe, and to do what you know is in your heart.

Feed your wolf. Make him strong.

CWd

I stuffed that letter into my bag, nestling it safely with Natalie's letter, then left the house and strode into the bright morning sunlight.

I checked my phone as I walked, and saw that it was 8:15. Hoping the repair shop that had current custody of my car was open, I walked the mile or so there, my most pressing need being a rental car. When I arrived they were open; after a twenty minute wait, I exited the parking lot behind the wheel of a near-new Dodge Journey. Two blocks later, while stopped at a red light, I grabbed my phone and punched in a text: *Good morning. Are U there?* I hit send as the light turned green, and in five minutes was at my destination, the Drury Inn.

I parked, made my way inside, and took the elevator up to the third floor. When it stopped and the doors opened I turned down the hall and made my way to room 318, hoping I could knock on the door and feed the right wolf. As I neared the room, however, I saw the housekeeper's cart in front of the door, the door itself wide open. I poked my head inside and called out, "Hello?"

A young woman in a maids' uniform came to the door. "Yes, can I help you?"

"The woman who's renting this room, do you know where she is, is she here?"

The maid shook her head. "I think," and she looked at her notepad affixed to the cart, "yes, this room is vacant, the person who was in here checked out this morning."

God damn it. God fucking damn it. That's what I get for waffling, for making a safe decision intended to hurt the fewest people possible. Only one person got hurt. Me.

I turned and headed down the hall, leaving the maid to continue her work. All I could think of was that yesterday I really had wanted to hold on to Leannette, to commit to something, to start the future now. It was, as the old man said, the fight between two wolves, and I had agreed to leave her here, and then the accident occurred which simply allowed me to fall into old, bad habits and feed the guilt. The choice I made late yesterday, I made it because I didn't want anyone to feel bad. No, let's be specific here: I didn't want my mother to be angry at me. I didn't want to repeat my past mistakes. I didn't want to add to the people in my life who are disappointed in me.

But the truth is that the only person who I was disappointing, the only person who wasn't forgiving me, is me. I was the sole being standing in the way of me being happy. I was the one who constantly chose to feed the wolf of doubt, guilt, resentment.

The elevator arrived and the doors opened. I stepped in, turned, hit the button for the lobby. As the doors slowly closed, I shook my head. This was a mess of my own doing. This was all my fault. This was . . . no. Forgive yourself, Natalie wrote. Forgive yourself. Do not feed the guilt. Which sounded great, but right now, at this very moment, what did it mean?

Of course. It meant that as soon as I was outside of this tin box, *SEND A DAMN TEXT TO LEANNETTE!!* It meant the "moment" was gone, but the future was still in front of me.

The elevator stopped and the doors opened. I stepped out and grabbed my phone, launched the Text app, and was about to start a message when I heard a voice.

"Wade!"

I stopped and scanned the lobby. Sitting on a bench near the door, suitcase at her feet, was Leannette. I didn't say anything, but ran toward her. She stood, and I paused a moment, then threw my arms around her in a warm hug, one that I decided then and there I never wanted to let go of.

"I just checked my phone and saw your text," she said. "What's up? What's going on?"

"My god," I said, "the last day, . . . you wouldn't believe." I let go of her and looked at her. Her coat was on, her bag at her feet, she had checked out and was sitting by the door of the hotel. She was obviously on her way out. "Wait, where are you going? Is everything okay?" Before she could answer I kept talking. ""Listen, about yesterday, I've been thinking, I mean, what I really want, what I wanted the whole time . . ."

"Wait wait wait, hold on a sec, okay?" she said. I stopped and nodded.

"Listen," she said, "yes, I checked out, and you know why?" I nodded no. "Because I called Uber, and was going get a ride and head down to Sedona to find you. But it's apparently a good thing he's not here yet, because you're not there." I nodded no again. "So what's going on, why are you here and not there?"

I first told her about the car accident. "Oh my God, are you okay?" Leannette threw her arms around me again and hugged me with such force that I felt the pressure of my injured muscles tighten. I put my arms around her as well, and we stood in lobby holding on to each other until the revolving door ushered someone into the lobby past us.

"My god," she said, "why didn't you call me or text me?"

"I didn't think it was that serious, . . ."

"Didn't think it was serious? Jesus Christ, are you crazy? You were almost killed."

"Yes, but I wasn't," I said, "and I really didn't want this to seem like, oh here I left you a few hours earlier and now here I am at your door because I've had a revelation. We wanted time, and I wanted to give you time."

"But something that serious, you should've let me know."

"Yes, I know that now. But that wasn't all of it. Here, come over here." I led us to a small love seat at the far end of the lobby, away from the door and the people. We sat down, and I told her about my phone call with my mom, the drive back to Flagstaff, the car breaking down, my evening with Carl Whitedog, and the letter from Natalie.

"So, after all that," I paused, . . . "after really seeing, maybe for the first time in my life that I can remember, that I have to live for myself and not for what I'm afraid everyone else will think or feel, here I am."

"Well, I'm happy you're okay, and I'm happy you came back."

"And here's, here's the thing." I took a deep breath. "Listen, when I was sitting there on the side of the road yesterday watching them take away those two people who died, it made me really, really aware of how there are no promises in life, no guarantees that if I make plans for tomorrow, or next week, or next month, I get to keep those plans. You know? Nothing but now, right now, today, here . . .that's all we're promised, that's all we can work with, that's all we get.

"And then last night, both the time with the old man artist and then reading that letter from Natalie, and how both of them, independently of one another, were steering me toward finally forgiving myself, not making decisions based on how much guilt I'll feel . . . that really made me think of all the things I've done, all the decisions I've made, that weren't for my happiness as much as they were for my avoiding feeling any pain or guilt. I wasn't going anywhere, I was just hiding.

"And I'm tired of spending so much time, so much of my life, saying okay to people getting what they want now with an eye toward me getting what I really want later on. It's, it's, . . . it's getting me more pissed off the more I think about it, all the time wasted looking backward, or worrying about what might happen next, instead of looking at life right fucking now.

"And if you feel that I'm being too emotional about this, or putting any pressure on you, well, I'm not, but I'm also not going to feel bad about it, I'm so damn tired of feeling bad about how everyone else feels." I paused and took a deep breath. Her hands were on mine, and she was looking directly at my eyes. "I don't want to bank on tomorrow any more, and I tell ya what, when I was climbing out of my car all I could think about was you, and I'm sorry but I really don't want to let another day pass without seeing if there's an us to be had, if that makes sense. I just want to argue . . ."

"I agree with you," she said, "you don't need to make any argument, because I feel the same way."

I stopped speaking and looked at her. "You do?"

"Oh my God," she said, "didn't you hear what I said a few seconds ago, that I checked out of this hotel so I could head to Sedona to find you and be with you? It's ironic, but I read about that accident on a news app last night, and all I could think about was, 'I hope he wasn't involved, I hope he's alright, I want him here, I don't want to wait to give him a hug, I don't want to wait for anything.' I was afraid that if it did involve you that I might have lost you, lost what we could be, maybe lost something great, . . . what if this is it, you and I, this is 'the one' for each of us? I don't want to leave that chance to tomorrow or next week or some other time."

"Really?"

"Damn it, no," and she engulfed me in a hug. "I'm not willing to lose someone just because I wanted to take time to think and ponder and wonder."

We held each other, and I could feel her body shaking with tears. I held her and stroked her hair. "I'm not going anywhere," I said, "At least

145

not now, not until we give this a chance."

When we let go of each other, I could see her eyes were red. "We're not crazy, are we?" I asked.

"Maybe," she said, "but I'm not willing to risk my heart to logic, not now."

"So head to Sedona, the two of us? No second thoughts?"

"None at all. I'm eager to get there, see Sedona, and see your place. It sounds nice from what you said."

"I think it should be fine for us. I mean, I got it thinking it would be just me, but it's not that small. I'm thinking of it as cozy, but enough room for both of us."

She smiled. "Sounds great, I cannot wait."

I grabbed her free hand with mine. "And like I was saying," I continued, "two-bedroom place, so room for us both."

"Oh so after all of this, after these epiphanies we both had, you're going to banish me to the spare bedroom, huh?" Her eyes were glowing, her smile devilish and playful.

"I was making no assumptions, my dear," I said, "and I'd rather not push things, and just let things grow at their own speed instead of forcing things to move quickly. I'm making no assumptions regarding living arrangements and where anyone sleeps, that sort of thing."

"I know," she said, "I trust you, your intentions, your feelings on this. And I trust mine, too. And even though in some ways it still feels awfully quick, it still feels right, and I don't want to waste a day."

I nodded. "Is it fast? Yes. Does it feel too fast? Actually, no, not really. I feel like, I don't know, . . . like we were supposed to be here together, it just took us longer than expected for us to find each other and get here, a couple of detours, but now we're where we belong, does that make sense?"

"It does," she said, "and that's really how I feel about all this as well, but there's this little voice, deep inside my head, telling me to slow the hell down. And of course the voice sounds like my mother, so . . .

"But I still want to do this, and like you said take it slow, figure things out as we go along, and just see what life brings. But at the same time I want this to begin now, I want us to begin now."

"Here's to making it up as we go along," I said.

She took a sip coffee, and said, "So everything so far, your life, Sarah, moving out here away from family, all that, do you have any regrets? Any feelings like, 'damn, I shouldn't have done that, wish I could have a do over,' anything like that?"

I pondered that for a moment, then replied, "I, . . .I don't really know, I don't know if you could call them regrets. I mean, do I wish I had done some things differently in hindsight? Sure, who doesn't, but I don't think I spend time regretting what I've done, or what I haven't done, roads not taken and all that. Why?"

"I just, . . . I just don't want you get involved in this, us, as if it can help make up for something you did wrong earlier, or something you wish you had done, you know? I want you to be comfortable and sure and happy doing this because it's this, not because it represents something else. Does that make sense?

"Yeah, I think so," I said, "and I understand that, and I appreciate you thinking about that, but my focus on my life, right now and hopefully for a long time to come, is on the future, not the past."

"Good."

"I need to stop thinking about and worrying about the past, and stop thinking I have to do things to 'make right' things that I've done. I mean, the whole 'feed the right wolf' thing, then the letter from Natalie, those things really hit me, and opened my eyes to, well, . . . to me, I guess, and how I am with people, how I am in relationships, and I think some of the times and issues I've had with Sarah kinda feed into the same thing, that I can't be, no matter how responsible I may feel, I'm not responsible for everyone being happy and put together and fulfilled, I guess. I need to focus on me, being the best Wade I can be. And take what I've learned from all those experiences and craft my life incorporating all that so I don't make the same mistakes or fall into the same bad, destructive habits."

"Oh God, you have no idea how good that makes me feel to hear you say that," Leannette said, "and believe me, I'll support you in whatever you need to do to keep making that happen."

"Thanks," I said. "What about you, any regrets, reconsiderations? Going into this for the now, not to make up for a previous transgression?"

"God, how biblical," she said, laughing, "but no, I'm not doing anything, . . . I made mistakes, we all do, but they are what they are, and they helped me become who I am, and to be honest I kinda like who I am right now. But no, no regrets, nothing that keeps me up thinking,

'God, if only I hadn't done that,' or nothing that makes me do things to make up for the past." She sipped her coffee again, and continued. "What's done is done, can't change it. All I can impact and control is what lies ahead of me, and what I do next."

"Damn," I said, "for someone supposedly getting over a bad relationship, you're pretty damn emotionally healthy."

She laughed again. "Okay, sure, I am today, but I reserve the right to be a blubbering idiot of emotions and hormones at any time, but I also promise not to take out yesterday's life on you, since you weren't part of it."

"Fair enough, and same here. Uhm, with the yesterday's life, not the hormones."

"You goof," and she playfully slapped my arm. "Let's get out of here."

"Oh yeah, you get to see my rental. And how symbolic is this: it's a Journey, a Dodge Journey."

"You're kidding, right?"

"Nope." I smiled. "Sometimes I think there's a force out there choreographing all of this, and this was the icing on the cake."

"Too funny," she said. "Let's go."

We drove 89A from Flagstaff. This time I was aware of the beauty and tranquility and richness of it, not lost in thought. We took our time, even stopping a few times along the way in order to take in the splendor with childlike eyes. We took photos that would never do justice to reality. We stared in quiet awe at the hundred mile views. We listened as hawks and eagles soared above us, the only sound being the almost imperceptible whoosh of air through and around their wings. We opened ourselves to every sensory experience available, and soaked in every moment.

I stopped for a moment where the accident happened yesterday. Other than skid marks on the road, there was no telltale sign of what had happened, the lives that had ended. Like smoke in the wind, it was gone. No trace.

"You okay?" she asked.

"Oddly grateful," I replied. "I want to remember this spot. I want this spot to be the place where my life turned into what it is today, and hopefully every day going forward." I turned and kissed her cheek. "I want to remember this, the tragically ugly and the breathtakingly beautiful, because this is where in many ways I feel like I was finally born."

"It was that powerful, what happened."

"Yeah."

"Well then," she said, laying her head on my shoulder, "let's make sure we do this place, and the accident, justice."

We drove on, and entered Sedona from the north, 89A taking us directly into the downtown area marked by furious tourist activity. We slowly moved through town, each of us pointing out items of interest – hey, look at that red cliff! Look, jeep tours! – until we found our turn just south of the downtown area. We swung west on 89A and continued another half mile to the older, less touristy west side of Sedona, the neighborhood where my condo would be found. I followed the direction on my phone GPS, and we were there in minutes, arriving in front of a cute adobe building of two stories that looked to hold maybe 6 or 8 units, all surrounded by stone landscaping dotted with cacti, set against a fortress of immense red and purple rock formations that stood guard over that part of town.

I pulled into the lot, and Leannette said, "Oh, this is gorgeous, this is beautiful," as she looked around, trying to catch every site and save it to memory. "Wow, you found this on the Internet? Nice."

"Lucky," I said, "really, the Internet pictures didn't do this justice." I turned the car off. "The owner said he'd leave the keys and info in the real estate office next door, . . . which, yeah, there it is. Want to come with?"

"Yes yes," she said, and she quickly unbuckled her seatbelt and climbed out of the car, her newest adventure about to begin. I did the same and we walked across the lot to the office. Since I had pre-wired the money for the first two months and emailed a signed copy of the lease, there was nothing for me to do except give them my car info and driver's license number for verification, and get the keys. That done, we hurried back to the car, grabbed some bags, and headed to our new place.

It was a first floor unit on the far end of the complex. We entered into the living room; it extended back to a dining area, and the kitchen was off to the left. A large sliding glass door opened the dining area to a view of the hills and mountains to our west. To the right was a hallway, leading to both bedrooms and the bathrooms. To the left from the living room was a small room, not much more than an extended closet, which I guessed was the den, or what in "real estate marketing speak" passed as a den.

"Oh Wade, this place is darling," Leannette said as she walked in, looked around, and placed her bags down. "You didn't say it was furnished, this is nice."

"It's only partially furnished," I said, "Just a couch and table, the little dining set, kitchen's stocked with everything we need, and then there's a bed and chest in the bedroom, which . . ." And I stopped, thinking about what wasn't there. "Uh oh," I continued, "just one bed, one bedroom set, nothing in the extra bedroom." I turned and looked at her. "Sorry. We can get something else right away, I promise."

"You worry too much," she said, and galloped off to see the rest of the place. While she was checking out the bedrooms and bathrooms, I went into the kitchen. It was simple, functional, clean – perfect for what I wanted. I opened a few drawers and cabinets to see what was there, and was satisfied that life could continue with minimal effort. Leannette came back into the kitchen, excited look on her face. "There's even a patio off of the bedroom, this place is great."

"Yup," I said, "I think this is gonna work just fine." I smiled at her, and she gave me a quick kiss.

"Let's empty the car," she said, "and see what else is around here."

So we got going, getting the remainder of items out of the car, which didn't take too much time. We hung up some clothes, figured out where the laundry was (closet between den and kitchen), made sure the electricity and water were running (it was; I arranged for it to start Sunday, just in case I made it early), and made sure all the keys worked in the locks. When we were pleased with our first bit of progress, it was time to explore the area.

"How about some lunch? Oh, and hey, let's find a drug store, there's a few items I need," she said. "Can you look up a CVS or something on your phone?"

I pulled out my phone, went to Google, punched in CVS, and was met with 4 results. The first one made me stop and look for a moment: the corner of Route 179 and Schnebly Hill Road. Hmmm. Where had I seen that name before, Schnebly? I thought for a moment, waved it off, and then said, "Okay, we have 4 options, let's see what we find first."

Before we could leave my phone rang, the tone identifying the caller as my mom. I clicked to answer. "Hey Mom."

"Wade, how are you, did settle in to your new place yet?"

"Yeah ma, had to make a detour yesterday, but just got here, unloaded the car, and now off to run a few errands and pick up a few things, groceries, stuff like that. How are you doing, any news on the condo yet?" I covered the phone and mouthed the word 'Mom' to Leannette, and she nodded.

"Oh," and she took a deep breath followed by a sigh, "I'm fine, you know, getting along just fine with my one kid still here, but I'm sure you're doing well, and the condo, they still haven't let us back in yet, but Ruth from downstairs called and said they'll probably start letting people in by Thursday to get some things, so that's good, and in the meantime I'm staying with Beth and Aaron, but you knew that."

"Yes, I did," I said, "and you, you're okay? Healthy, all that?"

"Oh me, I'm fine, don't you worry about me."

"Okay mom, I won't. And mom? I'm glad I'm here. Coming here, it was the right thing to do."

"Oh, you're just excited to be there, someplace new, you just wait, you'll be missing all of us soon enough."

"I might be," I said, "but that doesn't change that I'm glad I came down here, and glad I made this change in general. Mom?"

"Yes dear?"

"I know you miss me, and really didn't want me moving down here, but I'm not going to feel bad or guilty about it. This is right, for me. I gotta do what's right for me, and this is it."

She was quiet for a moment, then said, "Well honey, all I really want is for you to be happy, that's what's most important."

"Thanks," I responded, and gave Leannette the 'thumbs up' and a nod. "Still love you, will always love you and worry about you, but this is good for me, so be happy for me, okay?"

A silent second, and then, "If this is what you need to do, then this is what you need to do, and I'll be okay with it. I'll miss you, but we'll talk each week, right?"

"Something like that, ma."

"In that case, I'm fine. You enjoy everything out there."

"Thanks mom. Hey, something else, I have a question for you, have you heard the name Schnebly before?"

"What's that?"

"Schnebly, the name. S-C-H-N-E-B-L-Y, Schnebly. There's a road with that name down here, and for some reason it sounds familiar."

"Oh, you know, that sounds like something that might have been my grandmother's maiden name, before she was married, at least I think it was something, Schnelly, Schable, something like that. Why"

"Just wondering. Like I said, I saw the name on the road and it rang a bell. Hey listen mom, a lot to do so I gotta run, but I'll call you later tonight, okay?"

"Call me tomorrow, Wade, I may be tired, and if that's the case I'll be going to bed early."

"Okay ma, love ya, call you tomorrow."

"Love you too, Wade, bye." And we hung up.

Leannette was listening. "What was that all about, Schnebly?"

"There's a road here, I saw it on the map looking for the CVS, and that name sounded familiar, I may have to look it up at some point or something. Anyway," I grabbed my coat, "Let's go."

We drove to the first CVS on the list, which was located just next door to a small stone building that looked straight out of a John Wayne western, marked by a large bronze sign: Sedona Historical Society. "Tell ya what," I said, "you find what you need in CVS, let me check out the historical society next door, okay? Maybe I can find out something about that name."

"Fine by me," she replied, "and there's a sandwich shop next door, I'll grab us something. You have any preference?"

"No, whatever looks good, I'm fine. I'll see you in a few." We exited the car and walked our separate ways. I crossed the lot and pushed open the rickety wooden door. There was one woman there behind the intricately carved wooden counter.

"Welcome," she said, "How can I help you?"

"Good afternoon, I was wondering, I saw the road, Schnebly, and I'm new in town, . . ."

"Oh, welcome to Sedona!"

" . . .thanks, I was wondering about that name, Schnebly. What or who was it, or is it?"

"Come over here," she said, and she stepped around from the counter and led me to a computer terminal perched on a desk near the back. She moved the mouse and the screen sprung to life. "Here, this page gives you the history of the town of Sedona, and then you can go to the Schnebly Home page and learn about the family, and there's even a link from there to their Ancestry page." She smiled and motioned for me to sit. "Short story, Sedona was named after the wife of the first settler here, Carl Schnebly, her name was Sedona Miller, but when she married it became Sedona Miller Schnebly." She pointed to the computer. "Go ahead, look into it, it's all right there."

I spent the next 15 minutes looking, reading, following links. I spent most of my time on the Ancestry site, looking over the family tree of Sedona, particularly following the chain for her daughter, Pearl. Funny, my great-grandmother – my mom's grandmother – was named Pearl. It wasn't so funny when I followed the chain and it ended at my name. It was past funny, all the way to holy-shit-what-the-hell-how-can-this-be astounding.

Just as I saw my name the bell attached to the front door jangled. I turned, and Leannette entered carrying two bags, one from CVS, another from the sandwich shop. She saw me as the woman behind the counter welcomed her, and she smiled, pointed at me, and made her way to where I was sitting.

"Hey, whatcha find?"

I looked up at her. "I, . . . I found myself."

"Huh? What are you talking about?"

I told her about Sedona Schnebly, the namesake of the town. "Remember when I asked my mom about the name Schnebly? And she thought her grandmother's maiden name was something like that? Well, it was exactly like that. Look." I pointed to the screen, and she leaned closer to see. "Sedona Schnebly is my great-great-grandmother."

"Your what?" she said. "You gotta be kidding, no way, that's too crazy." She leaned even closer, and I pointed and scrolled down the page and traced the names all the way to mine.

The woman came back over to us. "Did you say you're related to Sedona Schnebly?"

"I, uh, . . . well, I had no idea I was, but apparently I am." I turned and looked up at her. "Seems I'm a great-great-grandson of Sedona Schnebly, and I had no idea, none at all."

A smile lit her face. "Well then, my oh my, we're cousins! My name is Gloria Jordan."

"Cousin Gloria, nice to meet you. I'm Wade Benthagen." We shook hands. "This floors me, I moved here from Chicago, I mean we just arrived in town what, an hour ago? And I've never been here before, and now to find this, . . ."

"It was meant to be," Gloria said, and she smiled and walked back behind the counter. "Something was drawing you to your ancestral home, and here you are."

Leannette and I spent the next hour seated there at the terminal, eating our sandwiches, reading about the town and its namesake, and tracing the history of her offspring and family. It was after about 45 minutes of tracing family down Sedona's Ancestry tree that I made another discovery.

"Holy cats, look at this," I said to Leannette, and pointed to the name on the monitor.

"Who's that, . . . wait, is that your friend . . ."

"Yup, same first name, same last name, same year and location of birth. Gotta be."

"Oh my God." She turned toward me and started grinning. "Jesus, it's a good thing nothing ever happened between you two."

"Man, I've gotta call her tonight and tell her, she's gonna freak out, she'll never believe it."

"You have a few calls to make tonight, don't you? Her, your sister, your friend Dan, . . ."

"Well yeah, and you need to call your mom, and it might be nice to check up on the couple who drove you to Albuquerque, oh, and your brother."

"Suddenly so much to do," she said, "we made it and now we need to let the world know we've landed." She placed her hand on my shoulder. "You need to let the world know that you landed where the world, where fate, destiny, karma, whatever, wanted you to land. God, what are the odds. Oh, hey, wait a minute," she said, "I thought you said Sedona meant 'peace,' but the woman said it's someone's name, what's that all about?"

"Well, honestly I had no idea what Sedona meant, but to me it meant peace. It meant beginning anew. It represented peace. So in a literal sense, no, it doesn't mean peace. But to me it does."

She nodded quietly, then said, "You're playing kinda fast and loose with the etymological rules here, but in this case I can accept that. That works for me."

Gloria spoke from across the counter. "You should head over to the Public Library, there's a bronze statue of Sedona Schnebly there. Her great-granddaughter was the model, they looked remarkably alike." She smiled as she was talking. "It's a beautiful sculpture."

I turned to Leannette. "Looks like next stop is the library?"

She smiled and moved her face close to mine. "I know you want to soak up every bit of this, but it'll be there tomorrow. Maybe we should get some groceries and head home and turn the place into something habitable first?"

I smiled back, kissed her, and said, "You are so right. Sedona was there for years before I even knew about her, it'll be there for a while longer, . . . and so will I. We can check it out and, heck, even get library cards tomorrow. Let's go home."

She kissed me back. "Let's head home."

We both got up from our chairs. "Thank you, cousin Gloria, for all this information, and it was so nice meeting you, and hopefully we'll see you again."

"Oh that would be nice, stop by any time," she said with a big grin. "Come back and I can update the local Schnebly family ancestry database with you and your address in it!" She waved and went back to her papers she was reading at the counter. And with that I took hold of Leannette's hand and we left, heading for our new home.

We stopped on the way home to pick up some groceries, and the quick stop turned into almost $200 worth of food stuffed into four bags. A couple hours later we were home, kitchen stocked, clothing put away as best as possible, and a few items set up to make it feel more like a home than just a few random rooms. A bottle of wine stood open on the kitchen counter, two glasses of pinot noir making their way to our waiting and eager hands. We plopped on the couch together, clicked glasses, and sipped the reward for our arrival and our afternoon of turning a house into a home.

"What a day this has been," Leannette said, her red curls falling randomly across her forehead and shoulders. "Actually, what a few days this has been."

I turned and said with a silly grin, "What a long strange trip it's been."

"Ha," she said, "strange, odd, unexpected, fun, frightening, interesting, . . ." she leaned and kissed my cheek, "and hopeful, and warm, and oddly inspiring and optimistic. It's like everything that existed before last week really doesn't exist anymore, like life kinda started new in New Mexico."

"Yeah, it does feel like that," I agreed, "I wasn't sure what to expect, I knew it would be different, I had no idea it would change to this extent."

We smiled at each other, clinked glasses again, exchanged a quick kiss, and sipped the wine. Which somehow caused my phone to ring. I looked at it. Dan.

"Take that, talk to him, tell him about everything," she said, "I'm going to organize the bathroom," and she got up and headed to the bedroom.

I answered and spent the next 30 minutes talking to Dan, bringing him up to speed on everything since Missouri. I told him about my mom's condo burning down, which elicited the expected "Holy crap, is she okay," then I spend a lot of time on Albuquerque, Leannette, the accident, the old Navajo artist, how we ended up together in my place in Sedona, and about my out-of-left-field discovery that I'm a descendant of Sedona Schnebly, the town's namesake. He was mostly quiet, other than the well placed "holy shit," or "you gotta be kidding me." When I finished, he was as worn out from listening as I was from the actual trip.

"So what now," he said, "I mean, after a couple of days you two are living together, already? Dontcha think that's kinda pushing it?"

"Like I said, for right now we're living in the same place more than living together, two bedrooms, all that. We both want to see what's here between us, we both think something is, and we don't want to waste any time thinking or waiting for the right moment. But we also both know ourselves, and know we need to take it slow and be sure. So for now, yeah, we're both here. And like I said, man, you'll love her, you gotta come down to visit maybe after Christmas or something, but you gotta meet her, you do that and you'll understand why the connection between us was huge and intense and immediate."

"This isn't Sarah 2.0," he said, "please tell me you're not rushing into something, someone, just to avoid the void of Sarah not being there, that this isn't just an attempt to make work what didn't before."

"Nope, not at all," I replied. "This stands on its own. I've come to terms with Sarah, us, what we were, how it ended. It was what it was, and I'm okay with myself and how it played out. I'm good. In fact, I'm better than I've been in years."

"Well that's good," he said.

"Oh, wait, best nugget last," I said. "When we were looking through the ancestry stuff where I discovered I was related to the real Sedona,

Feeding the Wolf

guess what else I found out?"

"Uhm, you're also related to Santa Claus?"

"No, no, . . . I traced a few different arms of Sedona's kids, their kids, and I found a name . . . Elena Rogers."

"Elena? Our Elena?"

"Yup, same year of birth, from southern Indiana, I'm pretty damn sure. Looks like Elena and I are distant cousins."

Silence, followed by, "Good thing you guys never, . . ."

"Yeah, no kidding, a little too 'Deliverance' if that had happened."

"You gonna tell her?"

"Oh yeah, I'll call her, if not tonight then tomorrow, I owe her a call anyway."

"Gonna tell her about Leannette?"

"That I might wait for," I replied.

"That might be best for her," he said.

We talked for a few more minutes, I made sure he had my new address, and then we signed off. Just as I did so, Leannette came out from the bedrooms.

"Bathroom is in order," she said, "at least it's in some order, you can rearrange your stuff the way you like." She refilled her empty wine glass then came back to the couch. "Food? Dinner?"

"We need some, but I'm wiped out."

"Me too," she said, "I was thinking more of finding someplace that delivers, pizza, Chinese, whatever, and do that. Too tired to go exploring tonight."

So that's what we did. We searched Google, found a Chinese place about a mile away, The Mandarin, that delivered. Just under 30 minutes later we were eating our first dinner in our new home; Kung Pao chicken and shrimp, pork fried rice, beef low mein. And we did so talking, talking about what tomorrow would look like, both the immediate tomorrow of Wednesday, and the long term tomorrow of next week, next month, next year. We talked of our fears, of neither of us wanting to repeat mistakes from the past, but also how neither of us felt that what we were doing now, here, with each other, was being done out of repentance for things done in the past. We both felt emotionally healthy, both of us for the first time in months, and we both thought it was due to our being able to look forward rather than constantly reviewing the past for our errors.

Later, we were sitting out on the back patio looking at the multitude of stars that littered the sky. She had a sweater wrapped around her shoulders, and I was just strumming my old acoustic guitar that had made the trip in one piece. We weren't saying much by then; we didn't need to. It was more than enough to be there together, under the majestic night sky, looking up and feeling that even though we felt incredibly small, we both felt incredibly hopeful and peaceful. I started strumming a Bruce Cockburn song, one of the few I knew, but one that seemed to fit the day and night perfectly.

"That's beautiful," she said, "I didn't know you could sing."

"If you'd really been listening you'd know I can't," I said, and she reached over and slapped me.

"It was fine, it was nice," she said. "Did you write that?"

"No, Bruce Cockburn, he's a Canadian singer-songwriter. That song, 'Child of the Wind', I don't know, it's always resonated with me, and tonight moreso. It just feels right."

"It does," she said. She looked at me and put a hand on my thigh. "This all feels right. I still sometimes wonder if it shouldn't, but it does, so I'm not going to fight it." She got up. "It's cold, I'm tired, I'm going to bed."

"It is late," I said, "I could use some sleep as well. You take the bed, I'll take the couch."

"Okay, stop," she said, and she stepped close and put her arms around me, her face inches from mine. "What I'd like is to fall asleep with you next to me, holding me, or me holding you, but to feel you there," she said, "I would like that very much, but I'm not sure I'm ready for anything more in there than that right now, if you get what I'm saying."

"I do get what you're saying," I replied, "And I would also love to just fall asleep with my arms around you. And I can wait for anything else until it's right for you," I kissed her, "or right for us." And I kissed her again, her left hand holding the back of my head, her right hand pressing hard into my back.

When out lips parted, she looked into my eyes, and for a brief moment it felt as though she were possibly looking into my soul, and said, "Let's go."

Two Years Later, Sunday, October 17

I came out to the patio where Leannette was holding her, the two of them wrapped in a warm blanket, Leannette's hands clasped tight around the baby, her right wrist adorned with a silver and turquoise bracelet. I sat next to them on the rocker that we had purchased just after moving in. We rocked for a moment, and I looked at her, and looked at the baby.

"Heard from mom, she made it back home okay," I said. "And Beth and Aaron and Julia are staying the night with her, so all is good."

"That's great," Leannette said, "I'm glad they were all able to come out for this."

"Well, not every day your granddaughter gets baptized," I said, and I looked at the tiny pink face peeking from the blanket and said to it, "isn't that right, Caitlin? Isn't that right, you little punkin', you."

"And my mom and Kyle and Lauren all made it back to their hotel, he texted me," Leannette said as she wrapped the blanket more tightly around the baby. "We're getting together for breakfast tomorrow before they head back to Phoenix to catch their flights."

"Sounds perfect," I said, "Actually, this whole day has been pretty perfect."

I looked up, and out at the sky full of stars. From our first night here Leannette and I had spent so much time out here, looking up at the heavens, talking, asking questions of each other and ourselves. It had been not only our release but our therapy, and ultimately our redemption and our promise to the future. It took us about 3 weeks to realize we were in love, and then another 6 months until we decided that our futures lie intertwined with each other. We had a simple wedding, Dan coming down for it along with her brother Kyle and his wife

Lauren. Nine months later we learned that our twosome would become a threesome, and now we're the parents of a beautiful baby girl, Caitlin, all of 5 weeks old.

I kept working as a writer, getting the same marketing and advertising work as I had in Chicago. In fact, most of my clients kept me, seeing that from where content is written doesn't matter much, and that me writing from my home office in Sedona wasn't any different from me writing from my home office in Chicago. What did change was that I started doing more creative writing, both at the prodding from Leannette and from my own personal need. It felt right, and it felt necessary. It started with me just randomly writing, free-form thoughts, ideas, almost confessional, definitely therapeutic. From there it became moments in time, captured emotions that presented themselves as short poems. I actually sold a few of those, which was completely unexpected as I never had any formal training in creating poetry. I had studied creative writing, so when I started writing short stories it was a natural progression – and it felt right. As it did when I started a novel. Sure, everyone wants to write a novel, but not everyone does. But I figured, why not? And again, it felt right.

Leannette kept working for her company as a designer of distance education courses, but she found herself increasingly disillusioned and left that after eight months. She followed her heart – once again – and started working for the Sedona branch of the Arizona Humane Society, and was soon managing their retail store and adoption center in town. She spent her days surrounded by, and caring for, animals that needed her. She was in her element, doing what she was meant to do.

My mother's condo wasn't able to be saved after all, but she received a fantastic insurance settlement from it. What she did with it was surprising, but then again maybe not too much: she bought a small patio home in Sun City, Arizona. She would be here during the winter months, along with her sister, my Aunt Joan, and in the summer they lived in the Chicago suburbs at Aunt Joan's house (which was plenty big, since she hadn't moved when her 4 kids left home, and had kept it still even after Uncle Greg died). So my mom had the best of all worlds: half the year near her daughter and her family, and now half the year somewhat near her son and his family. The two-hour driving distance was perfect; not too close, but easy enough for a Sunday visit.

When I ended up speaking with Elena about how we were distant cousins, she was incredulously in denial, probably stricken with fear over the thought of spending years trying to seduce a relative. Eventually she did her own research and found the same as I did, and our relationship became one of close cousins and friends. When I told her about Leannette she was happy for me, with the same initial reservations that Dan held (and for that matter that Beth held, and my mom, and everyone who knows me), but she was genuinely happy that I had found happiness. It was made even sweeter when she announced, just before the baptism, that she was engaged to someone she had met the night of my going away party. Full circle, I guess.

I spoke to Amy in Springfield a few more times after I arrived In Sedona, but eventually our correspondence trailed off, our only commonality being the death of a beautiful woman who left us both far too soon. I held on to the letter from Natalie for a while, and shared it with Leannette, and I used it as a reminder to look forward, and to forgive myself and be good to myself. Eventually I gave it to Leannette and asked her to get rid of it, that I didn't want to know how she did it or what she did. She told me it was gone, and I've never asked about it. But I'll never forget it, and I'll always think of the note, and the evening I read it, as just another step in the rebirth of my life, another guidepost pointing toward a better future that I was due.

Inside our home, on the large wall behind the sofa, hung a painting, something purchased by us on a weekend trip to Flagstaff. I probably knew, as soon as I saw it, that someday I'd own it, and now I did. Carl Whitedog didn't seem surprised at all when we came to his studio looking to purchase it, and he was kind enough to provide a personal inscription on the back. And now, every time I enter that room and see the images, I remind myself to keep feeding the right wolf, the one that fills a life with love and happiness.

All the others in life – Dan, Beth, Aaron, Kyle, friends, family – kept living their lives, kept prospering, and kept learning from mistakes. Isn't that what we all do? Isn't that the basic definition of life? Live and learn. And live some more.

I looked back to Leannette and Caitlin, and smiled, thinking how lucky I was, and remembering that luck in many cases was created as much as it was received. Yes, the timing of being in that gift shop in rural New Mexico was blind, random luck – but all else was the result of being open to life, to love, to happiness. I was open because I started to finally believe that I deserved happiness, but it was up to me to make my own happiness. I had finally learned . . . Pavlov would have been proud.

I looked down again at Caitlin – the beautiful package of happiness and joy that I had a hand in creating. And I looked up at Leannette, the beautiful woman who's been on the voyage with me for the past two years. And I looked up at the stars, the constellations light years away, and thought about how something out there wanted me to be right here, right now, and how I was open to making it happen. And how I'm still making each day happen, only now doing it on the best foundation I can create. No regrets, no excuses. I'm home.

Feeding the Wolf

Brian C. Holmsten

Made in the USA
Middletown, DE
07 September 2018